Walter Hook

A History of the Ancient Church of Porlock and of the Patron

St. Dubricius and his Times

Walter Hook

A History of the Ancient Church of Porlock and of the Patron St. Dubricius and his Times

ISBN/EAN: 9783337336813

Printed in Europe, USA, Canada, Australia, Japan

Cover: Foto ©Raphael Reischuk / pixelio.de

More available books at **www.hansebooks.com**

A HISTORY

OF THE

𝕬ncient 𝕮hurch of 𝕻orlock

AND OF THE

PATRON SAINT, ST. DUBRICIUS,

AND HIS TIMES

BY THE

Rev. WALTER HOOK, M.A.,

RECTOR OF PORLOCK ; PREBENDARY OF WORMINSTER, IN THE CATHEDRAL
OF WELLS ; AND RURAL DEAN.

LONDON :

MESSRS. PARKER & SON, 6, SOUTHAMPTON STREET, STRAND ; AND
BROAD STREET, OXFORD.

MESSRS. W. DAWSON & SONS, LIMITED, CANNON HOUSE, BREAM'S
BUILDINGS, CHANCERY LANE, E.C.

CHICHESTER : J. B. WILMSHURST, 21, EAST STREET.

Local Publishers.

MINEHEAD : -S. COX, THE BAZAAR AND LIBRARY, 1, PARK STREET.

WILLITON : COX BROS., PRINTERS, &C., LONG STREET.

To

The Right Reverend and Right Honourable

Arthur Charles,

Lord Bishop of the Diocese of Bath and Wells,

This Book is Dedicated

With deep respect and sincere affection

By his Son and Servant in Christ,

W. Hook.

CONTENTS.

ILLUSTRATIONS.

PREFACE.

ABOUT thirteen years ago Mrs. Halliday, of Glenthorne, being much struck with the beauty of the
great Monument in Porlock Church, determined to
investigate its history. There had always been a
tradition handed down from sexton to sexton that
the Effigies were those of a Lord Harington and
his wife, the Lady of Porlock. But neither Colinson,
the Historian of Somerset, nor Savage, in his
"History of the Hundred of Carhampton," knew
anything of it, and the former speaks of it as the
Tomb of a Knight Templar, though he does not
explain how a wife happened to be there! But
investigation proved the truth of the tradition, as is
shown in the beautifully illustrated volume entitled
"The Porlock Monuments," now, unfortunately, out
of print. After the publication of this book, my
cousin, Mrs. Halliday, handed over to me the
papers, copies of records, etc., which she had
collected in the course of her investigations, for any

future use. Many of these are embodied in her book, but some appear now for the first time. That portion of the work relating to the Chantry has been especially useful. It was written by Mr. Overend, of the Public Record Office, and I have to thank Mr. Overend for kindly revising the proofs in that part of this book.

I have to give thanks, also, to Mr. Roscoe Gibbs, for his Drawings of the Effigies on the Monuments, and of the Easter Tomb, which are reproduced from the "Porlock Monuments"; to Mr. E. Buckle, to the Rev. F. W. Weaver, and to Mr. C. E. H. Chadwyck-Healey, Q.C., whose advice and assistance have been invaluable to me, and to whom I am further indebted for the views of Porlock and the Old Chapel at the Weir.

W. H.

PORLOCK RECTORY,

July, 1893.

ST. DUBRICIUS AND HIS TIMES.

CHAPTER I.

HE period in which St. Dubricius lived has been ever the happy hunting ground, hazy with mystic antiquity, for poets and romancists. For it was the time of King Arthur and the Knights of the Round Table, of Geraint and Emil, of Launcelot and Elaine, of Sir Bois and the Quest of the Holy Grail—themes delightful to the bard, from the time of Geoffry of Monmouth to our own great poet of the "Idylls of the King." But the mists which afford pleasure to the romancist cause perplexity to the student of history. There is plenty of fancy but very little of fact. And there is no wonder at the confusion, when we consider that there was going on at that time the most terrible of all wars—a struggle for hearth and home, for very existence, against a fierce invader who, determined on conquest and new settlements, had "burnt his ships behind him." Round individual achievements, a bright halo may be diffused in song ; but of continuity of history there are but faint marks. *Cedant arma togæ.* The deeds of mighty men, their successes, their victories, their parentage, their position, were celebrated in saga and in song at the time, but fitted together afterwards, and transcribed in seasons of less turbulence, or in the calm seclusion of the cloister.

1

There are some of the ancient songs still in existence, but they only throw flashes of light upon the historical line, which has laboriously to be bridged over from one scanty fact to another, and straightened oftentimes by imagination or surmise.

The oldest known British historian, if he may so be called, is Gildas, who lived in the sixth century. Between him and the Saxon Bede there is a wide gap, for Bede was born in A.D. 673. But when writing was scarce, oral traditions had been handed down from father to son, in song or in tale, and the most probable of them were collected in the twelfth century in the "Book of Llandaff." In this are "Readings concerning the Life of St. Dubricius," giving a full account of the saint. The book was compiled about the time of the translation of the bones of Dubricius to Llandaff, which fact must have given it a great interest at the time. A little later than this, numerous other romantic and legendary tales were collected by Geoffry (or Jeffry) ap. Arthur, of Monmouth. Of course, St. Dubricius figures in this work in connection with King Arthur, but we rely rather on the more sober Book of Llandaff.*

St. Dubricius, Dubric, or, in Welsh, Dyfrig, was of royal birth. That indeed might not have been of great importance, when kings were numerous, and were little more than petty chieftains. *Primi inter pares* no doubt they were, but there were a good many of them. However, Dubricius' grandfather was Brychan, a British king, and his mother was Eurddil, "a lady of great quality," daughter of another British king, by name Pebiau, who ruled over the small district of Erchin, or Archenfield, on the Severn. In connection with

----

* See Appendix A.

his birth, the banks of the Gwain, near Fishguard, and the banks of the Wye, are mentioned. It seems most probable that he was born at Ynis Eurddil—so called from his mother's name—near Madley, then known as Mochros, or Moch-rhes, supposed to be the same as the present Moccas. He was said to have been miraculously conceived, and miraculously born, but that was not apparently a great distinction in those days; at all events, he shared it with King Arthur! His first work was scholastic, and it was eminently successful. He established a school at his native place, another at Henllan, that is "Old Church," now Hentland, on the Wye, in the district of Erchenfield,* and a large college at Llanfrawthir, or Lanfrothir.†. His fame extended throughout all Britain, so that there came to him scholars from all parts, and not merely young students, but also learned men and doctors, and St. Teilo is mentioned as one of those who attended at his college. There were no less than 2,000 scholars, "bred to divinity and human learning (*literæ humaniores*)." This was Dubricius' first great work, but he did not confine his work only to the college,—his sphere of usefulness was to be extended.

It is a matter of question whether Britannia Secunda, or Wales, was at that time divided into dioceses. It would appear from the little evidence we have, that it was not so. It was probably the influence of Dubricius backed up by the liberality of Meurig ap Tewdrig, that made a permanent see of Llandaff, whereas before there

---

* With regard to Dubricius' connexion with Erchenfield, see Haddan and Stubbs' Councils, I., 146-7.

† Rees (Essay on "Welsh Saints," 171-195) says that there were lately, on a farm called Lanfrothir, in Hentland, traces of former importance.

had been suffragans under one bishop, the Bishop of Caerleon—famed Caerleon, the city of the legion, the Isca Silurum of the Romans. Caerleon had no doubt from the first its bishop, who was supreme over Wales. It had been, and was, a very important place—the strong-hold of Roman power in Britannia Secunda. Giraldus speaks of it in terms of great admiration. He mentions its theatres, its temples, its palaces. *" Videas hic multa pristinæ nobilitatis adhuc vestigia, et palatia immensa— egregiis muris partim adhuc exstantibus,"* &c.,* and at the present time, in the little village on the river Usk, with a Great Western railway station, not far from the wonderful Severn Tunnel, may still be seen an amphi-theatre, and a collection of Roman remains.

At the Council of Arles, held A.D 314, three British bishops were present. The object of the Council was to settle the difficulty which had arisen out of the Donatist schism. Donatus had set himself up in oppo-sition to Cæcilian, the elected Bishop of Carthage. He had asserted that the Church was not infallible ; that it had erred in his time, and that he was to be the restorer of it. The controversy, or schism, lasted long after the Council of Arles, and involved such questions as the validity of baptism as administered by those who were without the pale of the Church, and evoked the cele-brated treatises of St. Augustine of Hippo. But the Council of Arles, however ineffectually, condemned Donatus, and the British representatives gave their vote on the orthodox side.

These representatives were Restitutus of London, Eborius of York, and Adelphius *" de civitate Coloniæ*

---

* " You may still see here many remains of ancient grandeur, and immense palaces with wonderful walls, still partly standing." Giraldus Itin. Camb. i, c. 8 ; Giraldus lived c. 1170.

Londinensium." The last word is puzzling. It is
taken by some to imply Lincoln—Lindum, Lindensium·
It is asserted in favour of this being the place that sent
the representative to the Council, that it was a colony ;
and that, as far as we know, Caerleon was not. But
it is also denied with regard to Lincoln. Camalodunum
is the only place known to have been a colony in the
proper sense of the word. On the other hand, Caerleon was, as has been said, a most important place, and
a centre. Moreover, as Canon Bright says, " Caerleon,
the traditional home of the martyrs, and the traditional
seat of the earliest chief bishopric in Wales, appears
more naturally to associate itself with the third delegate
to Arles, than a town within a short distance of York,
and in the province whose capital was London."* It
was over this see that St. Dubricius presided, and so
important was the position of the Bishop of Caerleon
considered, that later writers have called him Arch-
bishop. This, however, cannot be allowed as correct.
As Bishop of Caerleon, we find Dubricius in connection
with King Arthur, the hero of romance. But while it is
necessary to discard all the wild and fanciful legends
and fables which were collected by Geoffry of Monmouth, it is by no means to be supposed that Arthur
was a mythical personage. According to the romance,
leaving out the story of his magic birth, he not only
contends with the Saxons—this, of course, is reality--
but he goes far afield. Scotland is in distress. After
the batttle of Badon Hill he sets off thither. He
relieves Dumbarton (Alcluyd), which is besieged by the
Scots and Picts. Returning southwards, he visits York,
and is distressed, seeing "that city given to idolatry."

* Early English Church Hist., p. 9

So he destroys the pagan temples and their images, and restores the Christian churches far and wide. Ireland next occupies his attention, and he conquers it; and so on to Iceland. For twelve years the necessities of romantic tale require his peaceful stay in Britain. Then he makes great conquests in Norway and in Gaul, which take him ten years. He returns to Britain, and holds high Court at Caerleon, attended by a large number of tributary kings. Presently the Romans demand tribute.

> " Came in from Rome,
> The slowly fading mistress of the world,
> Great lords who claimed the tribute as of yore.
> But Arthur spake, ' Behold, for these have sworn
> To fight my wars, and worship me as king.
>
> .   .   .   .
>
> No tribute will we pay.' So these great lords
> Turn back in wrath, and Arthur strove with Rome."*

He collects a large army, and passes over to Gaul. He is of course successful, and is preparing to cross the Alps and take Rome itself, when news is brought of the revolt of Modred, who has allied himself with the Saxons, Picts, and Scots! He returns, fights two great battles, one on the coast of Kent, the other near Winchester; forces Modred to fly to Cornwall, follows him, fights his last battle—fatal to himself and his antagonist—on the banks of the river Camlan. But he does not really die: a dusky barge, with three queens aboard, wafts him away to the " island valley of Avillion,"

> " ' Where I will heal me of my grievous wound.'
> So said he; and the barge with oar and sail
> Moved from the brink, like some full-breasted swan
> That, fluting a wild carol ere her death,
> Ruffles her pure cold plume, and takes the flood
> With swarthy webs.   .   .   .   ' He cannot die!'"†

---

* Coming of Arthur (Tennyson).   † Morte d'Arthur (Tennyson).

But because Arthur is the hero of romance, it is not to be supposed that he was not a real person. The Saxons had advanced with steady and bloody strides. Aurelius Ambrosius, whose name implies his Roman origin, was, Gildas says, the first leader of note against the invaders. Natanleod, a mighty chief, fell in battle against Cerdic. Urien fought against Ida and his Angles, but he fell through the jealousy of a chieftain of his own side, Morcamb, whose treachery, according to Nennius, delivered him into the hands of his enemies.* But there was a check to the invader, and a check implying a strong and capable leader. And such a leader was Arthur, the heroic captain of the Britons - - their leader to victory — whose name was handed down to posterity as eclipsing all other names. Whether he was the son of Meiriac ap Tewdrig, or of Uther Pendragon (the title Pendragon being given to an elective sovereign, paramount over other petty kings or chieftains) by Igerna, is a mere matter of conjecture. But he started his warlike career about A.D. 500, and gained the predominance in 508 or 517.†

He was very successful, apparently losing in no battles. According to Nennius, ‡ he gained twelve victories over the Saxons, but the greatest was that of Badon Hill. The exact locality of this great battle is a matter of conjecture. One writer assigns it to Badby in Wiltshire;§ others to Bath;‖ but Professor Freeman, with greater probability, places it at Badbury, in Dorset.¶ Dubricius, or Dyfrig, was present at that crucial time,

* Nennius, c. 62.   † Comp. Owen (Camb. Biog) and Whittaker (History of Manchester).

‡ Nennius, 64.   § Whittaker   Camden and Turner

¶ Freeman's Old English History, p. 35

and encouraged Prince Arthur by his presence and his
speech.   He spoke "burning words" to the army
then assembled, and gave his blessing to Arthur, who
"bore the cross of our Lord three days and three nights
on his shoulders," and the Britons were victorious.   It
was said that 840 men were slain by the king himself
in that battle, but this is from our romantic friend
Geoffry, of Monmouth.   It was at this time, c. 517, that
Arthur was crowned with all due solemnity at Caerleon,
by the Bishop Dubricius.   Dubricius was the friend and
adviser of the king, and was summoned to solemnize the
marriage of the latter with Guinevere.   We may seem to
be going back to romance, but the following must be
quoted :—

> " Then Arthur charged his warrior whom he loved
> And honored most, Sir Launcelot, to ride forth
> And bring the Queen—and watched from the gates.
> And Launcelot past away amongst the flow'rs
> (For then was latter April) and he turn'd
> Among the flowers in May with Guinevere,
> To whom arrived with Dubric the High Saint,
> Chief of the Church in Britain, and before
> The stateliest of her altar shrines, the king
> That morn was married.
> And all that week was old Caerleon gay,
> For by the hands of Dubric, the High Saint.
> They twain were married with all ceremony.
>
>   .   .   .   .
>
> And holy Dubric raised his hands, and spake,
> ' Reign ye, and live and love, and make the world
> Other, and may the Queen be one with thee,'" &c.

We have been led on to Caerleon, and to Arthur,
but it is necessary to retrace our steps to consider
Dubricius' dealings with the Pelagians.   It has been
stated that three British bishops attended the Council
of Arles.   It is also probable that there were representatives at the great Council of Nicæa, A.D. 325;
at all events the British Church assented to the decrees

of the Council with regard to Arianism, and the time of
keeping Easter * ; and afterwards also assented to the
resolution of the Council of Sardica, A.D. 347, against
those who decried Athanasius.† At the Council of
Ariminium (Rimini), A.D. 359, British bishops were
present, and three of them were so poor that their
expenses were paid out of the Imperial Treasury.‡ Of
the orthodoxy of the British church there is also
abundant evidence given by such men as Athanasius,
St. Chrysostom, and St. Jerome.§

But this state of things was rudely shaken by the
heresy of Pelagius, which gained great ground in Britain.
Pelagius himself was a Welshman, his original name
being Morgan, which in the old language signified "sea
born." Thence he took his foreign name from the Greek
word for sea (πελαγός). His tenets were shortly : the
denial of the doctrine of original sin ; and the denial,
consequently, of the necessity of grace : from which
followed the conclusion, that there is complete free will
and therefore the possibility of a sinless man, without
divine grace. It cannot be supposed that the people
gave much heed to, or could well understand the niceties
of the arguments used on either side, but they were
ready (such is human nature) to join with one who set
himself up against the "powers that be."

Whether Pelagius was, as is asserted, a monk, or even
as high as the abbot in the Abbey of Bangor,| or

* Eus. Vit. Con iii. 19.
† Athan. Apol. c. Ari. 1. ; Hist. Ari. 28.
‡ Sulpicius Severus. *Hist. Sac.* ii. 41.
§ Athan. ut supra. Chrys. quod Chr. sit Deus, 12 ; Jerome
Ep. 146 ; and elsewhere.
Ussher, *Eccles. Brit.* Antiq cviii. Ban-gor, the great circle,
is an universal denomination for a congregation or monastery.
Lappenberg, i. 64.

2

whether his whole life was spent abroad is uncertain. But we have the testimony of St. Augustine, that he was a man of piety and learning,* and he certainly exercised great influence. His particular doctrines against the dogmas of the Church were propagated in England by Agricola, who was the son of a Bishop Severianus.†

There was little learning in the British Church at that time, and indeed Gildas speaks of the Clergy as inferior. " Britain," he says, "has priests, but they are foolish."‡

At all events, the British Church in their desire for orthodoxy, sent frequent messages to the Bishops of Gaul to come and help them. These were received favourably, and at a " numerous synod," Germanus, Bishop of Auxerre, and Lupus of Troyes, were appointed to "uphold in Britain the belief in Divine Grace," and they receiving the commands of the Church (as Bede tells us), " with all imaginable inclination," immediately set forth. §

The Gallican missionaries were most successful. The Pelagians had been popular. But now they realized the fact that they could not withstand the superior learning and untiring zeal of these Bishops. Therefore they determined to appeal to the popular vote, which they believed would be on their side, and so bring matters to

---

* De Peccat. Mer. et Rem. iii, 1. Augustine also wrote an epistle to " Pelagius, my lord, greatly beloved." (Ep. cxlvi.)

† Prosp. Aquitan. Chron. Bede i. 17.

‡ Gild. Hist. 26. Bede i. 22.

§ The selection had either been suggested or was afterwards approved by Pope Celestine. As Lupus is not mentioned by Prosper of Aquitaine, it may be that the Pope named one, and the Synod another. But Prosper would naturally overrate the influence and power of the Pope, and therefore we may suppose that Celestine "approved" the action of the Synod. *Prosper Aquit.* c. 21. Tillemont memoires, xiv 154. *Angl. Sax. Ch.* i. 8. Bright, 16.

a crisis. Trusting in their orators they challenged their opponents to a public conference at Verulam. The challenge was accepted; and though the Pelagians did their best to influence the people—who flocked in great multitudes to the conference—both by the exhibition of great pomp and ceremony, and by very specious reasoning, they could not answer the arguments of the Bishops. And then it is recorded "as for the people, they gave sentence in their acclamations—they shouted for Germanus and Lupus, and could scarce command their temper so far as to forbear beating the Pelagians."

Certain miracles alleged to have been performed at the tomb of St. Alban, and the great "Alleluia" victory over the Picts and Saxons on the borders of North Wales, in which Germanus and Lupus took a leading part, had a very powerful effect, and the heresy nearly disappeared. But only for a time; and another visit was paid by Germanus to Britain, accompanied this time by Severus, Bishop of Trier (Treves).*

Amongst others who were desirous to uphold the Church teaching in Britain, and to promote more learning amongst the clergy was, no doubt, Dubricius. But that he worked with Germanus, or was even consecrated Bishop by him, seems impossible. Bede's dates are evidently erroneous. He places the first Gallic mission in the year 446; but it was probably nearly twenty years earlier, that is in 429, when Germanus had been eleven years Bishop of Auxerre. The second visit was in 447, when Germanus was an old man. He died next year, on July 31, having been bishop thirty years and twenty-five days.† Hence the assertion that Dubricius was consecrated

* Constan. vit. S. German. i 24: ii. 2: Bede i. 20
† Constan. vit. S. German. i 19, et seq.

Bishop of Llandaff by Germanus in 470, falls to the
ground.* He was indeed consecrated Bishop of
Llandaff, but not by Germanus, and at a later date.
But he carried on the work which Germanus had
started not so much against the remnant of Pelagianism, but especially against the ignorance and apathy of
the British clergy, so bitterly complained of by Gildas.
To the schools which Dubricius founded and supported,
reference has already been made. But besides those on
the Wye he founded, or helped to found, collegiate
monasteries at Llancarvan, Caergorworn, and Caerleon.

According to Giraldus Cambrensis, Pelagianism was
not absolutely quenched after the second visit of the
Gallican missionaries, but revived. Even if this was the
case, the citadel of orthodoxy, through the energy and
work of Dubricius, David, and others, was not so weak
as it had been before ; and the extreme ignorance of the
clergy just referred to had been to some extent obviated;
so that foreign aid would not again be necessary. At
all events Dubricius summoned a synod, at which both
clergy and laity attended. It was held at Brefi, afterwards called Llandewi-Brefi (Llandewi meaning the
place of David), a small town about eight miles from
Lampeter, and formerly the Roman Lorentium.† Giraldus
gives an account of the synod. When all were assembled
it was found that David, who was renowned and revered
for his wisdom and piety, was absent. A messenger was
sent, but failed to induce him to attend. Then one
Daniel, with Dubricius himself, aged as he was, and
bowed down with cares, went to the learned man and
overcame his reluctance. He spoke : and whereas

---

* Rees' Essay on Welsh Saints, 171, et seq.
† Lewis' Top. Dict., Wales. Mansi. viii. 583. Collier (Eccles.
Hist) calls the place Brovi.

before the whole synod had been unable to convert the Pelagians, those heretics were at once convinced by St. David, who, though standing on level ground, made himself heard by the whole assembly. As the hearts of the people rose within them, so did also the ground on which the saint was standing, till it became a hill, on which afterwards a church was built in his honour.

But Giraldus is by no means authentic, and such evidence as exists of the proceedings seems to be against the supposition that the synod of Llandewi-Brefi had anything to do with Pelagianism.*

Wearied with the toil and trials of a long and eventful life, and craving for rest and retirement, wherein he could give himself up to calm communion with his Lord, Dubricius, after the synod of Brefi, withdrew to the Isle of Enlli, or Bardsey, there to end his days. He could do so with the more satisfaction to his mind, as he knew that in St. David he had a right worthy successor. He spent his declining years in religious exercises, and Giraldus gives us a pretty legend with regard to this. He was engaged in copying the Gospel of St. John, when the church bell aroused him, and he instantly left his work, and hastened to attend the service. When he returned, to his amazement and his joy, he found the page on which he had been at work finished in letters of gold. On his death bed he had a glorious vision of the ascended Saviour, and expired with the words, faintly murmured, " Lord, take me up unto Thee."

The date of his death is given by Geoffry of Monmouth, as A.D. 522 ; but according to more reliable authorities, such as the Welsh Annals (Annales Cambriæ)

---

* Haddan & Stubbs i p. 116.   Bright's Early Eng. Church, p. 30.

and the Llandaff Book (Liber Landavensis) the year of
his departure in peace was 612.

In the Liber Landavensis, it is stated several times
that Dubricius lived to an extreme old age—that he
numbered 150 years when he died. If this was the
case, it is not necessary to agree with the assertion
that Dubricius' time has been ante-dated in order to
bring him into connection with King Arthur. For if
the battle at Badon Hill was fought in 520, which is the
most probable date, and Dubricius was the bishop who
blessed the troops and crowned Arthur king afterwards,
and if Dubricius at that time was thirty years old (and he
might have been younger), it would imply that he was 122
years old at his death in 612. As this is by no means
impossible, as the Liber Landavensis dwells upon his
extreme old age, and as we may be sure that such an
energetic bishop as he was would have come to meet
Augustine when he came to these shores in 597, had
he not long before retired or have been incapacitated
by weight of years, we may take the connection of St.
Dubricius with Arthur as having in it certainly a basis of
truth. Perhaps in times to come it will be doubted
that a bishop in the English church of over 92 years of
age, in the year 1893, was as active as any bishop on the
bench (Bishop Durnford of Chichester), but the fact
remains.

We must conclude, then, that the date given of
Dubricius' consecration to Llandaff, A.D. 470, is altogether out of the question, unless we accept the date
of his death given by Geoffry, and adopted by Rees,
Collier, and others, as being in 522. This would render
impossible his work recorded in the Council of Brefi ;
and it appears certain that Dubricius died at a very
great age in A.D. 612.

In 1120 the remains of St. Dubricius were removed from Bardsey Isle to Llandaff under the direction of Urban, bishop of that see.

It was with great difficulty, and after searching the oldest writings, that the bones of the saint were discovered. They were conveyed to the Cathedral, which had lately been rebuilt on the old foundations, and were there interred with great pomp and ceremony, and amidst general enthusiasm. It was probably at this time that certain churches were built and dedicated to God in the name of St. Dubricius. Three of these are near the Wye —at Whitchurch in the district of Erchenfield, in the county of Hereford ; and at Ballingham and Hartland. Some pious missionaries crossed the Channel and founded a church at Porlock, which is still called the Church of St. Dubricius.

CHAPTER II.

THE FITZ-ROGES CHURCH.

ABOUT 1280 years after the death of St. Dubricius, the church at Porlock dedicated in his name, to the honor and glory of God, had fallen into a dilapidated and deplorable condition. To this further reference will be made later on. For the present purpose it is sufficient to state that in the work of restoration, while two distinct eras in the fabric, one about A.D. 1200, and the other in the 15th century, are plain, traces were discovered of a somewhat earlier church. The remains of a wide arcade were found built into the north-west wall, of which the stones had evidently been under the influence of fire. Some of the stones also in the arch over the north-west door show signs of having been burnt. But it is im. possible to say how old this supposed previous church was. The probability is, however, that it was not built or commenced long before the Early English Church, which was erected by the Fitz-Roges family, or rather, according to tradition, by one member of that family, Sir Simon Fitz-Roges, the crusader.

That there was not a substantial building dating back to Saxon times seems almost certain when we refer to the history, scant though the details are, of the place.

Porlock, now known chiefly for the beauty of its scenery, and for its vicinity to the forest of Exmoor, where the wild red deer still find a shelter, and roam at large—their last home in England—was, it is asserted by the historian of Somerset, Collinson, and by Savage in his "Hundred of Carhampton," an important place in the olden times. But this does not seem to be borne out by fact. The assertion is made upon the ground that two attacks were made upon Porlock, by strong forces, which were resisted by the defenders—but this does not imply, as we shall see, that the defenders were only the people of Porlock.

A palace had been built here by one of the Saxon kings, situated, probably, to the west of Porlock proper, where afterwards a Manor house was erected. There was an extensive chace, which was in the Norman times, by encroachment, extended to the Royal Forest of Exmoor, and it may here be mentioned that in the time of Edward I. Porlock was disafforested with its woods, heaths, and appurtenances, according to the charter of forests, and entirely freed from the oppressive restrictions and penalties of the forest laws. (26 Edw. I.)

But the place itself was thinly populated, and the account given in Domesday Book shows that there were but 6 villeins, 3 bordars, and 6 bondmen.

Yet this small and thinly populated place was made the object of two attacks, or invasions, both notable, in one of which the invaders were beaten off with great loss, while the other was disastrous to the place and the neighbourhood. But in neither case were the few inhabitants left to defend themselves—the attacks were rather directed against Somerset generally than against Porlock in particular. The position of the place was favourable for the invader. The bay of Porlock is well sheltered with two bold headlands guarding it on the east and on the west. The coast has undergone many changes, and at one time the sea encroached considerably. There is a submarine forest reaching along the shore, which can still in many places clearly be traced. The flat alluvial land between

3

Porlock and its harbour, now called Porlock Weir, was apparently some 800 years ago a shallow and muddy inlet by which the light crafts of those days could make their way to the shore at high water. The sea has again receded slightly, but these flats are still known by the name of " the Marshes."

In the year 918 a Danish expedition was started from the coast of Armorica. Eadward, the son of the great Ælfred, a king of nearly equal eminence with his father as a warrior and leader of men, though far beneath him in culture and nobility of character,* was ready for the emergency. Fortresses had been built in various parts by himself, or at his suggestion by Æthelred, in various important places. The utility of these was demonstrated in the failure of this Danish expedition. After ravaging the coast of Wales, the Danish pirates attempted to penetrate into Herefordshire. They were opposed by the inhabitants, supported as they were from neighbouring strongholds, and suffered defeat. Driven into a wood, they were compelled to give hostages as a security for their leaving England for the future unmolested.

But Eadward was doubtful of their honour, and with the prudence of a foreseeing general lined the northern coast of Somerset with troops. His presage was right. The Danes made two attempts to land, one at Watchet, the other at Porlock, but they were defeated at both places with great loss. Of the two leaders, Earl Hraold was slain, and also the brother of Earl Ottar. The survivors fled to the Flat Holmes, an uninhabited island in the Severn, but want compelled them to abandon their place of refuge and to seek better fortune in Ireland.† Their descendants perhaps took part in

---

* Florence, of Worcester, 901.
† Ang. Sax. Chron., 190. Trans So.

another and more formidable attack which was made upon Porlock about 130 years afterwards.*

In the time of Eadward the Confessor, Ælfgar the son of Leofric the great Earl of Mercia, was the Lord of the Manor of Porlock, as of many other manors in Somerset and Devon. Powerful, and successful in his undertakings, Ælfgar did not inherit the virtues of his father Leofric and his mother the lady Godiva (Godgifu), who were celebrated for their boundless liberality to the church, and for their good deeds. Ælfgar and his sons, on the contrary, come before us as men in whom no trust could be reposed and were ready to sacrifice anything to promote their personal objects. Hatred and rivalry towards the house of Harold, the son of the great Earl Godwine, were at this time the chief motives by which they were actuated.

Godwine and his sons, in 1051, had been declared outlaws by King Eadward, almost without a crime and quite without a hearing. Godwine had, indeed, resisted some of the King's measures, though he does not seem to have been guilty of revolt. But the King's mind had been poisoned against the mighty Earl, by the foreign favourites with whom he had surrounded himself,—for Eadward was both by education and inclination a Norman at heart—and by whom he was guided.

Godwine himself fled to Flanders, there to await the

---

* Savage, in his " Hundred of Carhampton " (p 93), asserts that Collinson in his " History of Somerset " is wrong in stating that this was an incursion of the Danes. The attack was made by " Lidwiccians," he says, so called from " Lid " a ship and " Wiccian " to watch. But the etymology is doubtful Florence renders the words " butan Liddwiccan " by " absque Armoricano regno de provincia quæ Lidwiccum dicitur." The word may be derived from the British name for Britanny--" Dlydaw " ; or the norse " wik," a creek may be joined to " Lid." But the Lidwiccians were Danish rovers. (Lingard, 1 c. lv., p. 191.)

course of events. But his two sons, Harold (afterwards King) and Leofwine, could not bear their injuries with equal patience. In Ireland there were many towns peopled with Danish settlers, and thither they directed their course, determined to raise forces to avenge their wrongs. When the great Earl was gone from amongst them, the people soon began to realize their loss. He had been their friend; he had stood up for their rights. He had certainly his faults, but these were counter-balanced by his virtues. The Norman favourites of the weak king still had Eadward's ear; and Leofric and Ælfgar were jealous opponents. Still, when Godwine determined to return, England, as a rule, was ready to receive him. He began by making overtures of reconciliation to the King, but when these were rejected, there was nothing for it but a return by force of arms. What he chiefly sought for was to deliver England from foreign domination, and he gained his cause—gained it without bloodshed, save in one case, and that was at Porlock, and was not his fault.

Harold, as has been said, had gone to Ireland to get recruits, and fit out an expedition. He, with his brother Leofwine, got together a goodly band of adventurers, and with nine strong ships made for the English coast. He entered the Bristol Channel, and directed his course to the Devon and Somerset shores, though they probably knew that the men of those parts were not well disposed towards Godwine. The Earl Godwine himself would only go where he was assured that the people were well affected towards him. But it seems to have been different in the case of Harold, at all events in this instance. Might he not, in his young blood, have thought of some revenge on Ælfgar, who owned the property at Porlock? Otherwise, what would have been the good of attacking shores so remote? Then also, his sister Eadgyth (Edith) the Fair, the wife of Eadward, who had held the neighbouring Manor of Selworthy, had, on the disgrace of her family, been deprived of all her goods, real and personal. It was, indeed, no fault of the inhabitants of Selworthy that she was ousted out of the manor, but revenge knows no discrimination. At all events, the nine ships were directed to the Somerset coast of the Bristol Channel, and a landing was effected at some spot between Porlock and Porlock Weir.

There is a field which still goes by the name of "Hellbyes," and not many years ago fragments of swords and warlike implements were found there. For Harold did not land without opposition, nor was the opposition weak. Beacons had been lighted over the range of the hill-tops, which extend far and wide in the country. From the summit of Dunkerry, the highest point of Exmoor, where the remains of hearths in which beacon fires were formerly kindled may still be seen, an alarm might have been spread to the heights of Plymouth on the one side, and to the Malvern Hills on the other, though they are 150 miles apart. Numbers flocked together to resist the invasion of those whom they deemed their foes. A stout resistance was made, but an undisciplined force has little chance against a compact body of men well exercised and drilled together, and with nothing before them but to do or to die. Thirty Thegns, and a very great number of other people were slain. Harold burnt every building, and carried off what spoil he could get. It was a sad day, not only for the people of Porlock, but for the good fame of Harold.*

The story of Harold's conduct at Porlock is told by

* Freeman's Norman Conquest, II 310.

the chroniclers in different ways, according to their
bias for or against him and his family. But they agree
in thinking that the harrying and slaying, unless done in
self-defence, were discreditable. Professor Freeman, after
protesting against the way in which the Porlock story is
slurred over by Thierry and Mr. St. John, concludes his
note by saying : " This part of Harold's conduct cannot
be defended, and it ought not to be concealed. It is
enough that he wiped out the stain by his refusal on a
later day to ravage one inch of the kingdom which had
been given him to guard." Collinson says : " That not
many years before he undertook to write his ' History of
Somerset,' men of Porlock used even then (c. 1750) to
point out remains of buildings which had been burnt, as
they supposed, at the great foray of Harold."

About a mile-and-a-half south-west of the Church,
there are traces of an encampment of an oval form.
The entrance to it is on the south side, and the upper
trenches are very deep. This may have been thrown
up during the preparation for the invasion of the Danes,
but (more probably) it was dug on the occasion of
Harold's invasion of the place.

The utter destruction of all buildings at that time
precludes the idea of any part of the Porlock Church
dating before 1051.

In Domesday Book, Baldwin de Execestre is given as
the Lord of the Manor of Porlock. He was a notable
man, and a great favourite of William I. When the
Conqueror became, after a long and severe struggle,
Master of Exeter, he, as usual, determined to build a
Castle which should dominate over the place. A portion
of this work may yet, perhaps, be traced in the gate which
leads from the town. The command was given to Baldwin of Morles, also called de Brioniis, who was to keep

watch over the city, and hasten the building of the Castle.

Baldwin was the son of William's kinsman and early guardian, Count Gilbert, who was the son of Geoffry, Earl of Eu, whose father was Richard the First of Normandy. According to Du Cange, he married a daughter of an aunt of King William, whom Dr. Oliver calls "Albreda, the Conqueror's niece." Orderic, however, simply says that she was "*bona uxor.*" Baldwin was handsomely rewarded for his services and his good connections, as he received a vast estate lying wholly in the two shires of Devon and Somerset, in the former of which he held the office of Sheriff. He appears in Somerset as holding the historic lordship of Porlock. His estates in Devonshire fill eleven columns of Domesday Book. Among his many tenants—English and French, but chiefly French— his own wife is twice mentioned: "*uxor Baldwini tenet de eo.*" Baldwin had three sons, the eldest of whom, Baldwin of Redvers (de Ripariis, afterwards Rivers), was renowned as holding Exeter when King Stephen attacked and took the Castle.

One Drogo was the tenant at Porlock at the time of Domesday. The description runs thus : "'The same (*i.e.* Drogo, or Drew) holds of Baldwin, Portloc. Algar held it in the time of King Edward, and it paid gheld for three hides. There is land for 12 plough-teams. There are there 6 villans, and 3 bordars and 6 bondmen: 300 acres of wood, and 500 acres of pasture. It was worth four pounds when he received it. Now 25 shillings." In the Exeter Domesday, this Drogo is called Rogo Fitz Nigel. He was probably the ancestor of the Fitz-Roges.*

* See Appendix B.

The family of Baldwin intermarried with the noble family of Courtenay. "From a Norman baron," says Gibbon, in his account of the Courtenay family, "Baldwin de Brioniis, who had been invested by the Conqueror, Hawise, the wife of Reginald, of Courtenay, derived the honour of Okehampton . . . Their son, Robert, married the sister of the Earl of Devon; at the end of a century, on the failure of the family of Rivers, his great grandson, Hugh the Second, succeeded to a title which was still considered as a territorial dignity."

The Earls of Devon, of the name of Courtenay, have flourished from that time to the present day. And of the number, Edward, called from his affliction "the blind," and from his virtues "the good," was the father of the Lady Elizabeth, of whom mention will be made in the next chapter, and whose effigy remains on the great monument in Porlock Church. "The great family," says Gibbon in a note, " De Ripuariis, de Redvers, de Rivers, ended in Edward I.'s time, in Isabella de Fortibus, a famous and potent dowager who long survived her brother and husband." In times of peace the members of these great families resided in their castles and manors in the west, and some of their possessions were given to persons connected with them by marriage or for other reasons. Thus in process of time the Manor of Porlock was enfeoffed on the family of Roges, or Fitz-Roges. They resided in the Manor House at Worthy, to the west of Porlock; and it may have been then, in quiet times, as the times went, that a Church was built.

Mention has been made of the translation of the bones of St. Dubricius from Bardsey Isle to Llandaff Cathedral. This event, attended with considerable ceremony, took place in 1120, and excited considerable interest in South Wales, and other parts of the country. It is by no

means unlikely that at this particular time a Church was
built, or begun to be built, which was dedicated in the
name of St. Dubricius. It was, of course, thatched, and
when afterwards it was burnt, it was replaced, or built on
by the Early English Church. But this, however, is conjecture, the Early English Church is a fact. In the
time of Henry II. we find Anthony de Porloc holding
a knight's fee from Robert Fitz-Roges: and in 1189,
Simon Fitz-Roges, Lord of the Manor, paid a fine of
100 shillings for impleading his right to half a knight's
fee in Porlock, against Richard de Raleigh. This half
knight's fee was afterwards held by the Earls of Devon
as of the honour of Okehampton, as appears from the
inquisition on the death of Hugh de Courtenay in 1377.*

It is to this Sir Simon that tradition points as the
builder of the Early English Church, and there is a certain amount of circumstantial evidence which upholds
the tradition. Sir Simon Fitz-Roges was lord of the
manor about A.D. 1200 ; the style of the building cor-
responds with that date. Sir Simon was a crusader : the
effigy of a knight with his legs crossed lies in a circular
niche in the south-west wall of the Church, and this
monument has always been said to be that of Sir Simon.
The armour and the triangular shield are of the time
of Richard I. (*i.e.*, 1189-1199). The crusader's legs are
crossed at the knee, showing that he had been in two
crusades, or had been twice to the East. The armour
would show that he was in the third crusade, under
Richard ; in which case he would have returned about
1192-3. And if he joined the fourth crusade in 1204,
there would have been ample time for the building of
the Church between the two events. And he probably

---

* Inq p m , 1 Ric II . No. 12

began the work directly after his first return, as the arcade presents an early type of the architecture of the time.

Everything points to Simon Fitz-Roges as the founder of the Early English Church. But whether it were he, or other members of the family, who carried out the work, there is no doubt that it was a very handsome edifice. The tower may be even of earlier date, a relic of the supposed older Church, but the "lancet" west window tells its own tale, as does also the arcade. Moreover, on the south wall the cells of the Early English lancet windows were found at the restoration in 1891. These windows had been built over at a later period (1418), when the Harington chantry was made, and the windows were turned into the decorated style. In one window the form of what was built by Fitz-Roges is left as a matter of interest, but similar windows, or rather traces of them, were found in all those on the south side. Moreover, the south wall of the aisle, originally of Early English building, has three feet of later work on the top, which shows plainly that there was a "lean-to" originally from the roof above the arcade to the old or lower wall, and such "lean-to's" were characteristic of the Early English churches. The roof over the nave, though now quite new, is, it is believed, exactly on the same lines as that in the Fitz-Roges Church. One set of rafters was discovered amidst a dilapidated and patched up whole, which gave the original shape, and which has been strictly followed. Of this, mention will be made again. Another relic, which shows the care taken in the Early Church, is the piscina. It is a very beautiful one, with a trefoiled head, and double drain. It had been filled up with rubble and mortar in later times, but perhaps this was an advantage

in preserving it, for it is now in nearly as good a condition as when it was first erected nearly seven hundred
years ago.

It was evidently a grand church, and testifies to·the
munificence and piety of the Fitz-Roges' family at that
period.

After this date, we have several notices of the Fitz-
Roges' family. For instance, in 1310 the Bishop of the
Diocese, "at Whetcumb, juxta Frome," admitted George
Roges to the rectory of Porlock, the patron being Henry
Roges, filius. George seems to have had bad health, for
he had licence of absence in 1311, "at the request of
Robert Fitzpayne," and again in the following year, and he
died in 1317.* Just before 1306, Simon de Roges and
Isabella, his wife, held the manor of Porlock.† Then
came Henry,‡ above-mentioned : but this must have
been by some arrangement, for in 1317 Richard de
Birlaunde was instituted rector, the patron being Herbert
de March (de Morisco), in right of his wife's dower
(Isabella) derived from her first husband, Simon de
Roges. The "de Mariscos," or Moors, were lords of
the island of Lundy, and tales of piracy and outrage
were long connected with them. The lay subsidies paid
at Porlock were—from Robert de Mohun ii˙ iiii͏ᵈ ; from
Nicolas Clihet ii˙ ; from Isabella de Roges, R. Sporke
and R. de Bromhamp xii˙§ About this time the Church
probably began to fall into dis-repair, which brings us
to another era in its history.

* Register of John de Drokensford, Bp. B. and W. (Somerset
Records) pp. 37, 47, 64.
† Inq. p. mortem, 34 Edw I.
‡ Called in Nomina Villarum (Kirby's Quest, Somerset Re-
cords) Hen. de Rokes.
§ Exchequer, Lay Subsidies. Somerset Records, p. 246.
One of the Roges' family bought Dovery Manor in 1236-7
(Feet of Fines, p 102.)

CHAPTER III.

THE HARINGTON CHURCH.

In the time of Richard the Second, we find Sir Nigel Loring, or Loherin, "Chivaler," in possession of the manor and advowson of Porlok. He was the owner of possessions in Hertford, Buckingham, Oxford, Devon and Cornwall, as well as at " Porlok," and paid for his " Fine " no less a sum than £1000.* Sir Nigel, or Sir Neele, was descended from the celebrated Counts of Lotharingia, "*regnum Lotharii,*" or, as afterwards called, Lorraine. He was a renowned man, and did great service to Edward III. He was a friend and follower of the Black Prince, and in the naval fight before Sluys, in the year 1340, he behaved with so much valour that he gained his knighthood. In the year 1356, he was appointed a special attendant, or, as we should call it now-a-days, aide-de-camp, to the Black Prince, and was with him at the battle of Poictiers, when he received acknowledgments for his prowess, and also rewards from the Prince for his service that day. A pension of £50 for his life was granted to him. But that campaign did not see the end of his service, for he was also present at the battle of Najara some ten years later. He was also the twentieth knight who received the honour of the Garter, and his plate of arms still remains on his stall in St. George's Chapel, Windsor.† He obtained a

---

* Feet of Fines, Divers Counties, Rich. II., No. 118, dated 27 Jan., 1384-5.
† Ashmole's Order of the Garter, c. 26, sect. 1.

EFFIGIES OF THE HARINGTON MONUMENT.

charter from the king for a market and fair at Porlock, and also a licence to make a park there.* How Sir Nigel Loring came to be lord of the manor of Porlock, is uncertain, but probably it was by marriage. He was the son of Roger Loring, and Cassandra, daughter of Reginald Pirot. He married Margaret, daughter and heiress of Sir Ralph Beaupel, of Landkey, Devon. Her mother was also an heiress, being the daughter of Elizabeth, who came into the fortune of Alan Bloyho. She had apparently been previously married to Stephen Tinterne. Sir Nigel had two daughters : Margaret, the younger, married John Peyver, of Toddington, Bedfordshire, son of Paulinus Peyver, Lord Steward of the Household in Henry III.'s time. Consequent upon alliances between the Peyvers, Broughtons, and the Earl of Bedford, the manor of Landkey descended to the present Duke of Bedford. The manor of Porlock fell to the share of Isabella, the elder daughter of Sir Nigel, who married Robert, third Baron Harington, of Aldingham. The first baron was Sir John, who was summoned to Parliament from 18 Edward II. to 21 Edward III. Robert was created a knight of the Bath at the coronation of Richard II., and died in 1406. At the "*inquisitio post mortem,*" held at Yevelchestre (Ilchester) in 1406, before Robert Grey, escheator, the twelve jurors found " that Robert de Haryngton, knight, held no lands or tenements in the said county, of the king in chief, but that he held on the day on which he died the manor of Porlok, together with the advowson of the church of the same manor, as of fee tail. Also that he held in his demesne as of fee four messuages, one carucate of land, thirty acres of meadow, and one

* Rot. Chart. 39 & 40, Edw. III., No. 10.

pound of cummin, with appurtenances, in Hunspylle, in the county aforesaid : Also that the aforesaid manor of Porlok, with the advowson, was held of Edward Courtenay, Earl of Devon, as of his manor of Oke-hampton, by knight service : And that the aforesaid four messuages, &c., were held of Fulk Fitz Waryn (who, being under age, was under the custody of the king). It was stated that the manor of Porlok was worth by the year, £20 13s. 4d., and the messuages, &c., £10 1s. 6d."*

The jurors found that Robert died on the 21st of May, and that John de Haryngton, "Chivaler," his son, was next heir, being of the age of twenty-two years and upwards. It is to this Sir John de Haryngton, who became the fourth baron, and to his wife, that the splendid monument was erected in St. Dubricius' Church, Porlock.

The family of Harington, or de Haverington, which thus comes into the history of Porlock, is of very ancient date, and, indeed, it is said that their descent can be traced to Elgiva, the daughter of King Ethelred.†

There were two branches of this ancient family, the Barons of Exton, and the Barons of Aldingham. But both came from the same stock, and both had members renowned as " Chivalers " of the highest order. Our Sir John was evidently in high favour at Court. In the year 1416, May 1st, Sigismund, the King of the Romans and Emperor elect, came to England on a visit to Henry V. The object of the visit was to put an end to the schism in the Church, where two popes were fiercely contending against each other, and to reconcile,

---

* Inq. p. Mort., 7 Hen. IV., No. 55.
† See Dugdale's Monasticon, vol. v., and the Charter Records of Holm Cultram Abbey ; Porlock Monuments, p. 5.

if possible, the Kings of England and France. King Henry, while anxious to receive his illustrious visitor with all due honour, was determined to show his independence, and sent his brother, Humphrey, Duke of Gloucester, the Earl of Salisbury, Lord Talbot and Lord Harington, to Dover to meet him. They rode into the sea with drawn swords, and desired information as to the intentions of the royal visitor, and whether he came claiming any jurisdiction in this realm. The answer was satisfactory. Sigismund was received, and was presently installed as a Knight of the Garter. The year afterwards we find Lord Harington accompanying Henry V. in his expedition to France, in which the leaders, besides the monarch, were the Dukes of Clarence and Gloucester, and with them the Earls of March, Warwick, Huntingdon, Suffolk, Salisbury, Lords Talbot, Edward Courtenay, Bouchier, and our Baron.* It was at this time that Henry dubbed forty-eight knights, and it would not be rash to assume that Lord Harington was one of them, if, indeed, he had not before this received the honour of knighthood, which seems most probable from his will.

He married Lady Elizabeth Courtenay, daughter of Edward, third Earl of Devon, and very early he and his wife planned, if not a restoration of the whole, at all events, a chantry in the old Church. This was evidently carried out, but not, perhaps, in his lifetime. The old lancet windows in the south aisle, which was the place for the chantry, were altered into windows of the decorated style, and it was at this time that the lean-to from the centre aisle was changed. Three feet of building were added to the old walls, in order that a wagon roof might be placed thereupon. And a beautiful

* Stowe's Chron., p. 358.

wagon roof it was. Rather more pointed than usual in
Somerset churches, it was very perfect in shape and
details.   The whole of the south aisle was recon-
structed at this time, but the moiety towards the east
end was much more elaborated.   For here was the
chantry of Sir John de Harington and his wife.   The
monument was afterwards erected in the centre of that
aisle, before the side altar.

The work was probably begun before Sir John's expedition with Henry V., and it is certain that it was
well carried out.   Sir John, Baron Harington, made his
will before he departed on the expedition with the king.
It begins thus : " In the name of God, Amen.   On the
eighth day of June, in the year of our Lord 1417, I,
John de Haryngton, knight, Lord de Aldyngham, being
of sound mind, and purposing by the grace of God to
visit foreign parts without the kingdom of England, do
make my testament in manner following.   First, I
bequeath my soul to God Almighty, to the Blessed
Mary, His Mother, and to all His Saints, and my body
to the nearest consecrated burial place wheresoever I
shall happen to die.   Also I bequeath to Elizabeth, my
wife, the half of all my silver plate, of whatsoever kind it
shall be."   To her also he bequeaths everything with
regard to house, butlery, bakehouse and stables, within
the counties of Somerset, Devon, and Cornwall.   If
there were any debts, he willed that his manor of Ugge-
burgh, in the County of Devon, should be sold.   But,
he adds, " if those my goods do suffice to pay all my
debts, then I will that my said manor, after my death,
be amortized to sustain two priests, as by the discretion
of my executors shall seem most expedient to celebrate
Divine Service, and to pray for the souls of my father
and mother, and of all my ancestors."   The rest of his

goods he leaves to his executors to "dispose and dis-
tribute in the manner in which, for the safety of my soul,
it shall seem best to them to be done, and to perform
other things which, in certain indentures, more fully
appear."

The executors were the Lady Elizabeth, his wife,
Thomas Baldyng, clerk, John Copleston, senior,
Thomas Broughton and John Russell, clerks. The
will was proved before Master John Estcourt, &c., on
the 26th of April, 1418.*

It was evidently when Sir John married the Lady
Elizabeth Courtenay that the idea of a chantry in the
church at Porlock was formed, but there was first a great
deal of work to be done. The beautiful decorated
windows, which were built on the old lancet windows,
as we have seen, tell the story. When Sir John de
Harington left England to join in the King's expedition to France, the work had been begun, and probably
had been well-nigh finished. It was to this that he
referred when in his will he spoke about "other things
which, in other indentures, more fully appear." He
endowed two chantry priests to pray for the souls of
his father and mother, and his ancestors, and he left
money for "alms to be distributed to divers poor
persons on the foundation of Sir John Harington."

He did not return from the French expedition, but as
to how or where he died there is no record. The
"*Inquisitio post mortem*" was held at Taunton on May
7th, 6 Henry V., when the usual forms were gone
through with regard to the lands and property of the
deceased knight, and it was stated that he died Feb. 11,

* There are indications in the will of an erasure about the
size of a crown piece

5

1418.   His widow, Elizabeth, became lady of the manor
of Porlock, with reversion to the heirs-at-law of her late
husband.   In the will of John Bakelyn, of Dunster,
A.D. 1420, which is amongst the records of the castle,
the lady is called " Lady Elizabeth Harington, Lady of
Porlock."*

But although Baron John died in 1418, the Letters
Patent which authorize the founding of the chantry, only
date from 14 Edw. iv., so that his wishes were not carried
into effect for fifty-six years.   This may account for the
later architectural style of the canopy over the monument.   Mention is made of the "Chapel of the Blessed
Mary" in the Church of Porlock, and of two "perpetual
chaplains," who were to celebrate divine service at the
altar aforesaid.†

The Lady of Porlock married again, and lived to a
good old age.   Her second husband was Sir William
Bonville, knight, who on 23 Sept. 1449, was summoned
to Parliament as Lord Bonville of Chewton, and on 8th
Feb. 1461 elected a Knight of the Garter.   In the
Inquisition after death, she is styled in one place, " Elizabeth Harington, widow," and in another " Elizabeth Lady
Harington, who was the wife of William Bonville,
knight."   Lord Bonville was executed after the second
battle of St. Albans (A.D. 1461), and attainted, so his
title is ignored.   But the Lady still was the "Lady of
Porlock."   When Sir William Harington of Aldingham
died (1457), the brother and heir-at-law of John, fourth
Baron, no mention is made in the Post Mortem Inquisitio of the Manor of Porlock—showing that it still
remained in the hands of the Lady Elizabeth.   The

* " Dunster and its Lords," by Maxwell Lyte.
† Patent Roll, 14 Edw. IV. part 2, m. 13.

only daughter, Elizabeth, of the above mentioned William, 5th Baron Harington, married William the son and heir of the second Bonville,* by his first wife ; and the inter· marriage (as the christian names are similar) renders the history somewhat confusing. In right of his wife this Bonville had, by courtesy, the title of Lord Harington.

Elizabeth Bonville died in her father's lifetime.† The heir was her son, the third Bonville. He married Katherine, a daughter of Richard Neville, Earl of Salisbury, and was the father of Cecily—a great heiress, as she was the only representative of the Harington and Bonville families. Amongst others the Manor of Porlock fell to her.

Cecily married Sir Thomas Grey, third Lord Ferrers of Groby, and son of Sir John Grey, the second lord, by Elizabeth, who after his death became the wife of Edw. IV. Sir Thomas' first wife was Anne, niece of Edw. IV. He was created Earl of Huntingdon in 1471, and Marquis of Dorset in 1475. By Cecily the marquis had fourteen children ; his grandson was the father of the unfortunate Lady Jane Grey. Cecily's second husband was Henry Stafford, second son of the second Duke of Buckingham of that name, by Catherine, daughter of Richard Widville, Earl Rivers. The duke was beheaded by order of Richard III. in 1483: his son, Henry Stafford, was created Earl of Wiltshire by Henry VII. in 1509, and was constituted a Knight of the Garter, being the 258th on the roll of the order.

It may be added as a matter of interest that Cecily,

---

* At the battle of Wakefield (1460) Lord Bonville, his only son (this William) and *his* only son were present. The two last were killed, the grandfather only escaping. The first was beheaded after the second battle of St. Albans.

† *Inquisitio post mortem*, 11 Edw IV., No. 64

Marchioness of Dorset, evidently stood high in the court
of Henry VIII., for in Sept. 1533, at the christening of
the Princess, afterwards Queen Elizabeth, daughter of
Anne Boleyn, according to Hall, "The old Marchioness
of Dorset, widow" was one of the child's god-mothers,
and in the grand procession the Marquis, her son, bore
the Salt; and she made a christening gift of "three gilt
bowls pounced with a cover." But this is taking us
away from Porlock.

The exact date of the Harington monument in the
chantry of St. Mary in the church of St. Dubricius
cannot be assigned : nor, as has been said, is it all of the
same date. The effigies were carved, and were in place
before the canopy was erected.

The monument stood originally in the south aisle (the
chantry chapel), and the old foundations were found
when the new pavement was laid down. To the east
stood the chantry altar, and the piscina still remains.
The knight is in plate armour : he wears the cuirass,
with a richly sculptured bawdrick round the hips; his
long sword is supported by a belt, falling diagonally from
the waist to the left side, the hilt being decorated with
the sacred monogram, and supported beneath by two
sculptured grotesques; the arms are protected by rere-
braces, fan shaped elbow pieces and vambraces, and the
hands by cuffed gauntlets; he has "his cuisses on his
thighs, gallantly armed," and sollerets to the feet; his
rouelle spurs are attached by buckle straps passing over
the insteps; he wears a collar and badge, and his
bascinet is encircled by a wreath, probably intended for
roses and rose leaves : his head lies upon a helmet,
composed of a lion's head erased—the Harington crest;
his feet rest upon a lion. The lady wears a mitred head
dress, richly diapered and encircled by a coronet of

fleur-de-lys : she is clad in a mantle fastened over the breast by tasselled cordons, and beneath this she wears the surcoat, and under this the kirtle ; she has a double chain round her neck, with a pendant and an ornamental girdle ; her feet rest on a boar—the badge of the Courtenays. Two other monuments similar to this exist—one at Bromsgrove to Sir Humphrey Stafford and his lady (1450) ; the other at Tong, to Sir William and Lady Vernon (c. 1467). These are so like the Porlock monument that they must, we may assume, have been by the same artist.*

As has been said, the date of the monument cannot exactly be given, but there is no doubt that the effigies are earlier than the canopy   It may have been that the effigies were sculptured in the lifetime of the Lady Elizabeth. It seems certain that they were in their place when the formal licence was given for the erection of the chantry (Patent Roll 14 Edw. iv.). With regard to the canopy there are in the spandrels repeated in a distinct manner three *torteaux*, the primitive arms of the Courtenays, as also of the ancient Counts of Boulogne, Kings of Jerusalem, and Emperors of Constantinople, with whom the Courtenays shared a common ancestry.†

It may have been erected by Cecily the heiress, of whom mention has been made above.

But though great pains were given to the elaboration of the chantry which had been begun by John, fourth Baron Harington, the rest of the church was not neglected, but the alterations were later. Whereas in the south aisle, where the chantry was, the windows are of the decorated style, those in the north wall are perpendicular, which

---

* Roscoe Gibbs in "The Porlock Monuments," p. 52.
† Porlock Monuments, p. 22

plainly shows that that part of the church was restored by Lady Elizabeth, or even later, by Cecily, Marchioness of Dorset. The church was evidently the object of great care. There is a fine "Easter tomb" against the north east wall of the chancel. Savage supposes that it was the ancient altar of the church; but it is hardly of a large enough size, nor has it the five crosses on the slab. In the centre panel, however, are displayed the five sacred wounds on a shield, and in the right corner is the sacred monogram; on the west face the chief ornament is a Tudor rose within a cinque foiled quatre foil; all the others are trefoiled; on the east end is a carved shield with other emblems of the Passion. This is given in Parker's Concise Glossary of Architecture as a specimen of an Altar tomb. But it is probably the base of the Easter Sepulchre. That there was a rood screen, there can be no doubt. The window which was above it still remains unaltered; three steps leading up to it may still be seen; there are marks in the pillars which evidence its existence; moreover, as will be seen presently, we have a record as to when it was taken down.

There is a small chapel at the east end of the church, which is now used as a priest's vestry. This is of perpendicular style, rather later than the windows in the north wall of the church. With regard to this various conjectures have been made. There is no piscina, and it would be too small for a Lady chapel. It was probably a sacrarium where were kept the sacred vessels and the vestments. These, doubtless, were gorgeous, and the traces of colour and decoration which were found in the church, chantry, and on the monument, show that the Harington church was very "magnifical."

EASTER TOMB.

CHAPTER IV.

THE PORLOCK CHANTRY.

AFTER the death of the Lady Elizabeth, the Lady of Porlock in 1471, there is every reason to suppose that the heiress Cecily, Marchioness of Dorset, kept up an interest in the place, and in the church. But these were troublous times. The terrible civil war that was going on with its fluctuations of success, between the parties of the Red Rose and the White, and which deluged the land with the blood of the noblest of her sons, was followed after a short period by the crusade against the possessions of the Church. That abuses and superstitions abounded in the Church before the time of the Reformation, which had gradually crept in, no one can doubt. And there were good and earnest men in those days who were anxious for the good of the Church, to purify the one and to abolish the other. There are, of course, different opinions as to their work; some asserting that they did too much, others that they did not do enough. But there can be no two opinions with regard to those who dealt with the temporalities of the Church. From the king to his lowest courtier, the object to each so-called "reformer" was that he himself should get as much of the prey as possible. They feigned to act under the banner of religion, but it was convenient to them to forget that money or land given or bequeathed for pious purposes, should to pious purposes be devoted, even if not to their original object; and not diverted into the possession or pockets of individuals. The monasteries were doubtless in a bad state, and required reform if not suppression. But the former would not pay, while the latter would, and the suppression of 376 monasteries supplied the king's exchequer with a revenue of £30,000 a year, and £100,000 in addition as ready money, the value of realized property confiscated—all of which had been left for pious uses.*

But this was over; the monasteries were settled. There remained, however, the cathedrals and churches for the hand of the spoiler. In 1535, an Act of Parliament had been passed (26 Hen. VIII., c. 3) for the payment of first fruits and tenths to the Crown. By it the first fruits, revenues, and profits of every bishopric, monastery, parsonage, chantry, or other benefice, etc., were for one year after presentation to belong to the king, and a grant was also made to him of a yearly tenth of the value of such spiritual livings and promotions. Commissioners were appointed to enquire as to the value of the benefices, etc., in each diocese, and the result of their labours is the record known as the Valor Ecclesiasticus.† Certain deductions were allowed, such as "rentes resolute to the Chief Lordes, and other annuell and perpetuall rentes and charges, which any spirituall person or persones, ben bounden yerely to paie to any person or persons, to ther heires or successors for ever, or to give yerely yn almes by reason of any foundacyon or ordynaunce, and all fees for stewardes, receyvours, baylyffes, and auditours, and synodes and proxis."

In the return made of the Monastery of the Blessed Mary of Clyve, or Cliff, by the Abbot William Dovell,

---

*Hook's " Lives of the Archbishops," vol. vi., p. 82.
*Printed by the Record Commissioners. Somerset Record. Soc. II., 49, 223.

one of the items is "an annual pension received from the Chantry of Porlock," which was allowed as a deduction.* But the next year the monastery was dissolved, and its revenues, including this pension, were received by the officers of the Exchequer.

The return for the two Porlock chantries in the *Valor Ecclesiasticus* is as follows (translated):

1535. William England and Robert Laurauns, Chantry priests there Two chantries there *per annum*, *viz.*, in Rents of Assize as well of the free as the customary tenants in Ugborough £20 : 4ˢ : 1ᵈ. And in the rent of a tenement, with the appurtenances in Dover-hayes 12ˢ. Perquisites of Court 10ˢ. [total] £23 : 16 : 1. [*Deductions*] : thereof

"In the fee of John Gylbert Steward there, 13ˢ 4ᵈ; in alms distributed to divers poor persons on the foundation of John Harington, knight, £4 : 6 : 8 yearly; and paid to the Rector of Porlock for a pension, 2ˢ 6ᵈ; and paid to the Lord of Luccomb for a chief rent, per annum, 8ᵈ; to the abbot of Cleve for procurations and visitations of the same Chauntries 10ˢ; and paid for rent to our Lord the King 5ᵈ; And there remains clear £18 : 2 : 6. The tenth thereof 36ˢ 3ᵈ."

But the chantries were not to get off so easily, and the next attack was to be upon them, and the properties they represented. These were very large, a fact which would doubtless have a great effect on the minds of those who calling themselves "reformers," realized that when confiscation took place there would probably be some "pickings" even for outsiders!

But apart from this, it seems that it was time that

---

* Ex T R . County Bags, Somerset. Bag of Miscellanea. No 1

something should be done to check the superstitions held with regard to those chantries. We have but to read the celebrated work of Sir Thomas More, the "Supplication of Souls," to see how strongly the doctrine of a penal purgatory had taken root in the minds of men of the day. The Holy Eucharist had come to be celebrated rather for the benefit of souls in purgatory, than as the sacrifice of thanksgiving, and communion of the Church Militant here on earth. An order of clergy had arisen whose office was that of offering up the Mass for this purpose. To many churches chantries were added, as in the case of Westminster and Tewkesbury Abbeys, where altars were placed in chapels built round the choir; but mostly, as was the case at Porlock, the chapels were screened off within the Church, between the pillars and the side walls. These, and the priests who served them, were endowed by the founders with the idea that the salvation of souls was rather connected with the intermediate state, than with this life of probation. So men of wealth got to think that no matter how bad their present lives were, they could, by giving or devising lands or money for erecting a chantry, and supporting a priest for saying masses for their souls, get out of condemnation hereafter.

In the last parliament of Henry VIII., an Act was passed, and commissioners were appointed for the purpose of enquiring into the tithes and value of the chantry lands, and other possessions (37 Hen. VIII., c. 4). Commissioners were speedily sent round, but the Act did not come at once into operation, in consequence of the death of the King. The following is the report of the Porlock Chantry.*

---

* Exchequer. Queen's Remembrancer. Church Goods. Somerset ₃b. No. 20.

𝕿𝖍𝖎𝖘 𝕵𝖓𝖛𝖊𝖓𝖙𝖔𝖗𝖞 indented made the 17th day of March in the 37th year of the reign of our Sovereign Lord King Henry the 8th &c. between Sir Giles Strangways Knight Thomas Denton and Roger Kynsey Gent. Commissioners appointed for the Survey of all Chantries, Free chapels, and other spiritual promotions in the County of Somerset assigned to our said Sovereign Lord the King's Majesty's disposition by an Act of Parliament made in the 37th year of his noble reign of the one part, and Sir Robert Laurence Chantry Priest of our Lady Chantry in Porlock of the other part, 𝖂𝖎𝖙𝖓𝖊𝖘𝖘𝖊𝖙𝖍 that there was remaining in the custody of the said Chantry Priest at the making hereof such goods and ornaments as hereafter followeth, that is to say :—

First a chalice of silver parcel gilt valued at 40ˢ·
Item a pair of vestments of old blue sattin valued at 4ˢ·
Item an old cope of black damask valued at 3ˢ·
Item an old pair of vestments valued at 2ˢ·
Item an old torn white cope valued at 2ˢ·
Item a pair of lattin candlesticks valued at 16ᵈ·
Item four altar clothes valued at 12ᵈ·

𝕬𝖑𝖑 which goods and ornaments abovesaid the said Commissioners have delivered unto the said Chantry Priest and have straightly commanded him safely to keep the same. 𝕴𝖓 𝖂𝖎𝖙𝖓𝖊𝖘𝖘 whereof to the one part of this Inventory indented remaining with the said Commissioners the said Chantry Priest hath set his seal and subscribed his name, and to the other part of this said Inventory indented, remaining with the said Chantry Priest, the said Commissioners have set their seals the day and year above written.

By me Robert Lawrens,
Priest.

We cannot but suspect that the worthy Lawrence, chantry priest, had hidden some of the vestments and ornaments for fear of their confiscation, for it is improbable that the well ordered, well appointed Harington chantry should after so few years show such a meagre set of things. This would not have been an exceptional case, for when the spoliation of churches took place, as it presently did, the custodians of church goods tried to save them, as was notably the case at Durham, where it was reported to the Privy Council that a quantity of treasure had been conveyed into the Dean's chamber, and though stringent orders were issued by the Privy Council, it is not improbable (says Blunt)* that the treasure never fell into the hands of the Crown, but is still concealed in some part of the cathedral. The Dean and Canons of Chester, for a similar offence, were even sent to the Fleet.

The Act of 37 Hen. VIII. was followed by another Act in the next reign (1 Edw. VI. c. 14) of a sweeping character, in which the former Act was recited. This was introduced into the House of Lords on Dec. 6, 1547, and was pushed on with such rapidity that the second and third readings were taken on the 12th and 13th of the month, and the Act was passed on the 14th. Cranmer, Bonner, and other bishops opposed it, but in vain. Cranmer did not deny that there were abuses connected with the chantries but, he said, however much abuse had been connected with these endowments, they were distinctly ecclesiastical funds, and ought not to be diverted from ecclesiastical purposes. The alienation of tithes to laymen at the dissolution of monasteries had impoverished the clergy, and the numbers of the working clergy had been greatly diminished at the same time, so that many parishes were now left altogether without pastoral care. It was right that the endowment of the chantries, when abolished,

* Hist. of Reformation, I. 348.

should be used for the maintenance of the parochial clergy, and the increase of their numbers, at all events for religious purposes. But this argument was not likely to hold good with the Lord Protector, the Privy Council, or the House of Commons, who saw here a good way of providing money for their expenses without voting any supplies by way of taxation. And the chantries were rich. In St. Paul's cathedral there were forty-seven, with average endowments of £25, with a quantity of gold and silver plate, and rich vestments. Here according to the value of money at that time was something like £12,000 a year, besides the ornaments. Other chantries were more or less richly endowed—and here was indeed a spoil! "How much the revenue of all these chantries, etc." says Fuller, "amounted to, God knows . . . . . Some of these chantries may be said to be in a double sense suppressed, as not only put down, but also concealed, never coming into the exchequer, being silently pocketed by private (but potent) persons." There was a regular scramble for these chantry lands, everyone getting what they could, and "as for those who fairly purchased them of the King they had such good bargains that thereby all enriched and some ennobled both themselves and posterity."

There were some wise patrons, who, foreseeing the coming confiscation, resumed or conveyed away the endowment of their ancestors, and were successful in avoiding the spoliation of the Privy Council. The Marquis of Dorset, Cecily's husband, was one of them, and took steps to empower his brother, Lord Grey, to enter upon the lands belonging to the Porlock Chantry. The Royal license was granted in 1547 (1 Edw. VI.) to Robert Lawrence and John Wollok, clerks, chaplains of the perpetual chantry of John, Lord Haryngton, and

Elizabeth his wife, in the parish church of Porlock, that they or their successors might give and grant to Thomas Grey, knight, Lord Grey, the brother of the King's dearest cousin Henry, Marquis of Dorset, the said Chantry of Porlock and all manors, messuages, lands, etc., belonging to the same, situated in the counties of Devon and Somerset or elsewhere, the grantee to hold the premises for ever upon payment of an annual rent of thirty-six shillings and three pence every Christmas, to the King's use at the Court of First Fruits and Tenths. This last charge was due to the Crown according to the return made in 1535 before quoted, in which the tenth is put down at the same sum. By this document also license was given to the Marquis of Dorset, and to all founders, donors and patrons of the chantry, that they might ratify and confirm this grant; and to the grantee that he should hold the said lands, etc., notwithstanding they had been conferred upon the Chaplains of the Chantry, to celebrate masses, or perform other like services.*

This was only just in time. It was dated July 15. On November 4, the Parliament was opened, and one of the first Acts was that which dealt with the remaining chantries (1 Edw. VI. c. 14). The preamble to the Act dwells on the errors and superstitions in Christian religion, "brought into the myndes of men by their ignorance of their veric trewe and perfect salvation through the death of Jesus Christ, and by devising and phantasinge vayne opynions of purgatorye and masses satisfactorye to be done for them which be departed, the which doctryne and vayn opynion by nothing more is maintained and upholden than by the abuse of trentalls, chauntries, and

---

* Patent Roll, 1 Edw. VI. pt. 6, m. 5 (36).

other provisions for the contynaunce of the said blyndness and ignoraunce." It proceeds to a proposed conversion of such institutions to "good and godlie uses, as in erecting of Grammar Schools, to the education of youths in virtue and godlinesse, the further augmentation of the Universities, and better provision for the poore and nedye." But as this could not be, in the present Parliament, provided and conveniently done, and as it could not be committed to any other than to the King's Highness—his Majesty with and by the advice of his Highness' most prudent council, can and will, both for the honour of God, and the weal of his Majesty's realm, order, alter, convert and dispose the same. This, of course, meant that the money obtained by the confiscation should generally go to the Privy Council and its needs. Grammar Schools were indeed founded, but the number was very small. A list of eighteen is given by Strype, but as many of the chantry endowments were associated with educating purposes, it is doubtful whether the new schools more than compensated for those which were destroyed.

Commissioners were again appointed who were to make certificate into the Court of Augmentations of all manors, lands, etc., assigned to the uses of chantries, which were to be placed under the control of the Court and the revenues received by its officers for the King's use.

Commissioners were sent to Porlock and the following is the return they made :—

Porlock. Too Chauntries foundyd within the parysche churche there Ar yerely worthe in Landes, tenemenes, and hereditementes, in the tenure of sondery persones, as maye appere particularly more at large by the rentall of the same   ·   ·   ·   ·   xxiij^{li} vj^s ij^d.

Wherof in Rents resolute paide yerely to sondery persones - · - - xvj⁸ ix^d ob.
And so remayneth clere - - xxij^li ix^s iiij^d ob.

Plate and Ornaments.

A Chalice of Silver guilte - - xiij oz. di. (½).
Ornaments praysed at - · - viij⁸.

Memorandum. Ther is but one incumbent ther whose name is Roberte Lawrence, clerke, having no certayne stipend for that he hathe (as he saythe) resigned the said Chauntrie to the Lorde Marques Dorsset a yere past and more.

The underwoodes and copses belonging to the saide Chauntries contayne xx^lio acres, praysed to be worthe every acre vj⁸ viij^d—vj^li xiij⁸ iiij^d, wherof was wonte to be solde and cut downe yerely ij acres.

Ther was distributed yerely to too poore men remayning ther, by the fundation of the saide chauntries, viz. to either of theym by the weke vij^d.—lx⁸. viij^d.

To a clerke serving in the saide ij chauntries by the fundation yerely for his stipend or wage liij⁸. iiij^d.

To the poore people ther yerely in breade and drinke in the tyme of the Anniversarie kept for the founders xiiij⁸.

Lyghts foundyd within the same parysche churche Ar yerely worthe in One howse ther nowe in the tenure and worthe in occupying of John Goulde, junr. iiij⁸.

Goodes and Cattall gyven to the mayntenance of obites within the sayde paryshe churche, *videlicet,*

Certayne houscholde stuffe remaynyng in the custody of sondery persons praysed at xlv⁸ iiij^d, and one kowe remaynyng in the custody of Petre Torre, praysed at xiij⁸ iiij^d.   lviij⁸ yiij^d.

Memorandum. The personage ther is of the yerely value of xviij^li, wherof Roberte Broke, clerke, is now incumbent.

Partakers of the Lordes Holy Sooper ther, CCLX persones.*

As this Act was retrospective, and Porlock Chantry had been in existence less than four months before the commencement of the Parliament in which it was passed, its possessions would at once have passed to the King had it not been for a clause enacting that all letters patent made by the late or present King, to any person, of any of the said chantries or of any lands belonging to the same, and all grants and conveyances thereof made by the assent or license, under the Great Seal of England, of the late or the present King, to any persons, by any chantry priest, warden, etc., were to be good and effectual in the law, and available as well against the king, his heirs and successors, as against the chantry priests and their successors, and the founders, donors, and patrons of the same chantries.

Though this clause would confirm the title of Lord Grey to the Porlock Chantry lands, yet they were included by the officers of the Court of Augmentation in the Rolls of the accounts of Rents charged upon their collector for the Deanery of Dunster, in which ecclesiastical district Porlock was situated. The collector returned that the chantries were claimed under letters patent of the King, by Lord Grey who had received the rents belonging to them ; as, however, his lordship had not produced his grant in evidence and obtained a discharge, the amount was again inserted upon the Roll the following year, but only to be answered to by the accountant with the same excuse in the " Super." This continued through Edw. VI.'s reign.†

* Aug., Certs. of Colleges and Chantries. Somerset. Roll 42, No. 56.

† Ministers' Accounts 1 and 2 Edw. VI. No. 44 ; and Rolls of subsequent years.

Then came the sad history of Lady Jane Grey, on which we need not dwell, except to state that the whole family were inculpated, though some were pardoned. But in the insurrection of Wyatt against the marriage of Queen Mary with Philip of Spain, the Duke of Suffolk, and his brother Thomas, Lord Grey, took part, were tried, found guilty and beheaded. All their possessions became forfeit to the Crown, and with them the title to the lands of the Chantry of Porlock. They were, however, still entered on the Minister's Accounts with the same excuse from the collector in the "Super," and continued to be so throughout the reign of Philip and Mary.* The explanation of this is that directly after the conveyance made to him by the priests, Lord Grey had parted with his interest in the Chantry lands.† Their value was then £22 9s. 4½d., as will be seen from the report made at this time.‡

The Manor of Ugborough—the most valuable of the Chantry possessions, had been conveyed by a deed of bargain and sale to one Thomas Williams—the lands in Porlock and Luccombe leased to George Kelly for the term of ninety-five years.

Poor George Kelly got into difficulties over this. In 1561-2 there is the entry in the Roll as before for Porlock, in the charge upon the accountant, and in the "Super" are the arrears of six-and-a-half years charged upon Lord Grey. For this, Kelly, his lessee, was held responsible.§ The net value of the lands was estimated at £23 2s. 4½d.

---

* Ministers' Accounts, 4 and 5—5 and 6 Ph. and Mary, No. 31.

† Ex. L.T.R. Memoranda Roll, 9 Eliz. Easter, No. 6.

‡ See Appendix C.

§ Ministers' Accounts, 3 and 4 Eliz., No. 32.

Three years afterwards, at this valuation, the arrears charged upon Kelly amounted to £254 6s. 1½d. He disputed his liability to pay, and alleged that the charge was excessive, as he only had a lease of a small portion of the chantry lands worth only £3 7s. 3d. a year. Judgment was given in his favour. But he was still charged with the rent he had agreed to pay Lord Grey, and which would become due to the crown in consequence of his lordship's attainder. The Crown officers made a charge not only for the sixteen years since Lord Grey's execution, but for the six-and-a-half years between the making of the conveyance and the beheading of the lord.* The rent is thus made up:—5s. a year for the rent of the Mansion-house of the chantry with a garden, and 66s. to be paid to Lord Grey, of which latter sum 4d. a year only was for rent, the remaining 60s. 8d. to be divided between two poor persons every Michaelmas, in the Parish Church of Porlock. There was a mistake here, as 60s. 8d. and 4d. make up 61s. not 66s.; but it was afterwards rectified.†

As after this there is nothing in the "Super" relating to Porlock, the difficulty with Kelly may be presumed to have been settled.

In 1572, William Stoning, one of the informers so numerous in this reign, discovered, as he thought, that the lease to Kelly for ninety-five years was void and of no effect. He thereupon obtained a lease of those lands for himself, the grant being made out for the term of 21 years.‡ The mines and quarries were reserved to the Crown; but the tenant was to have what was necessary for repairs, and also howsboote, hedgboote,

* Ministers' Accounts, 12 and 13 Eliz., No. 31.
† Ministers' Accounts, 20 and 21 Eliz., No. 31.
‡ Aug., Transcripts of Leases, 15 Eliz., No. 77.

fyerboote, ploughboote, and carteboote. But in 1583
(July 27) at the petition of Sir Thomas Wentworth, Lord
Wentworth, Letters Patent were made out to his nominees,
Theophilus Adams, gentleman, and Robert Adams,
citizen and grocer of London, granting to them the two
Chantries of Porlock, at the annual rent of 13s. 4d.* On
what grounds Lord Wentworth laid claim to the chantries
does not appear. He had received one of those
indefinite grants, common to the times, of all lordships'
manors, messuages, etc., which had escaped the notice
of the Crown, or been concealed. Probably he had been
led to infer that Lord Grey's title was invalid, as he had
not in the first instance produced his letter patent, and
received a discharge (see above). Some arrangement
was made. Stoning obtained a new lease on April 30,
1584, but he did not enjoy it long. In 1596 it was in
the possession of a certain John Amery for the term of
his life, with remainder to Helen and Mary Amery, his
daughters, for the terms of their lives respectively.†

After the attainder of Henry Grey, Duke of Suffolk,
and Thomas, Lord Grey, their estates and rights, as a
matter of course, fell to the Crown. Amongst them was
the manor and advowson of Porlock. The manor was
afterwards granted to the Rogers' family of Cannington,
but the advowson was retained. Edward Rogers died
seized of this manor in 1627. Sir Francis Rogers
was his heir, but Porlock was left to his second son
George, who was succeeded by his brother Henry.
In 1672, this Henry Rogers of Cannington having
bequeathed £600 for the benefit of the poor in
that parish, proceeds:—"Item, I give to the poor of the

<hr>

* Patent Roll, 25 Eliz. pt 4; No. 7 and 10
† Aug. Transcripts of Leases, 26 Eliz., No. 162; and 38
Eliz. 99. Ministers' Accounts, 33 and 34 Eliz., No. 32; 43 and
44 Eliz., No. 32; and 21 and 22 James I., No. 26.

parish of Porlock the like sum of £600 to be laid out
and employed by my trustees and executors for main-
taining of the poor there." In 1689 a messuage and
tenement known by the name of Nether Staddon, in
Winsford parish, was purchased with this money and
conveyed to trustees, who should dispose of the rents
thereof for keeping such of the poor persons of Porlock
parish who were dwelling there, and whose ancestors
were born there, but not any new incomers or intruders
that should come to settle there. On the death of three
or more trustees, others were to be appointed, chosen
by the rector, churchwardens, overseers, and most substantial inhabitants of the same parish, for the time
being. There is at present a full number of trustees.
Besides this a moiety of the rents and profits of certain
lands in Cannington, which were purchased with the sum
of £2350, were to be applied to the maintenance of
twenty poor persons, sixteen of these to be of the manor
of Porlock. The Right Hon. Sir T. D. Acland, Bart. :
the Earl of Loveiace ; C. T. D. Acland, Esq. ; G. W.
Blathwayt, Esq. ; the Rector of Cannington, and others,
are the trustees, and dispense the charity.

Henry Rogers left no son. His sister and heiress,
Mary, had married in 1631, Sir George Wynter, of
Dyrham, Knight. Their son John Wynter, who married
Frances, daughter of Thomas Girard, of Trent, Co.
Somerset, Esq., left no son, and his daughter and heiress,
Mary, married in 1686 William Blathwayt, Esq., of St.
Martins', City of London, M.P. for Bath from 1690 to
1710, and a Clerk to the Privy Council in the reigns of
Charles II., James II., William III., and Queen Anne.
The present Lord of the Manor of Porlock is George
William Blathwayt, Esq., of Dyrham Park.*

* Somersetshire Wills, 2nd series, p. 92. See Appendix D.

CHAPTER V.

THE INCUMBENTS OF PORLOCK.

IN 1533, Robert Broke, Brock, or Brocke, was appointed Rector of the Parish, by the executor of Cicely, Marchioness of Dorset, Sir William Blunt. But the next appointment, which did not occur till 1562, was made by the crown, and it continued to be from that time a "crown living." Robert Broke held the living all through the trying times of the chantry history, which has been given, but beyond that we know little of him. After the chantries had been abolished, and their revenues confiscated, a raid was made on the ornaments and plate of the churches. On March 3rd, 1551, it was decreed "that forasmuch as the King's Majesty had need presently of a mass of money, therefore commissions should be addressed into all shires of England, to take into the King's hands such church plate as remaineth, to be employed unto his Highness' use." This was ruthlessly carried out.

"They tore," says Blunt, "the lead from the roofs, and wrenched out the brasses from the floors. The books they dispoiled of their costly covers, and then sold them for waste paper. The gold and silver plate they melted down with copper and lead, to make a coinage so shamefully debased as was never known before or since in England. The vestments of altars and of priests they turned into table-covers, carpets, and hangings when not very costly; and when worth more

money than usual they sold them to foreigners, not
caring who used them, for "superstitious" purposes, but
caring to make the best bargains they could."* This
spoliation went on through Edward VI.'s reign; only the
fabrics, which could not be utilised, remained.

The Rector, Robert Broke, lived through all this, and
if he concealed any of the plate or ornaments of the Harington Church, they have not yet been discovered. He
resigned in 1562, and Arthur Saul was presented to the
living. The following is a list of the Incumbents of
Porlock.†

INCUMBENT.	PATRON.
1297. Walter - - -	Hen. Roges, fil.
1310. George Roges -	Hen. Roges
1314. Will. de Wergrave	-
1317. Ric. de Burlande	Herb. de Marisco
1349. Joh. de Speke -	Rob. de Stockleye
1361. Will. Lo Heryn	Nigel lo Heryn
Walt. Philip	
1420. Rob. Godde -	Eliz. dra de Harynton
1456. Ric. Ewyn -	Joh. Broughton, arm.
1458. Tho. Estyngton, M.A.	Will. Bonville, arm. de Tod-ington, dinc.
1471. Hen. Wold -	Joh. Broughton
1487. Tho. Harrisfin -	R. Marchis. Dorcestre
1491. Will. Morris, LL.D. -	Rob. Broughton, mil.
1519. Will. Brownyng	Ric. Lond. Ep. et complures alii feoffatores Hen. Stafford, Com. Wilts
1527. Rog. Trugge -	Joh. Trugge in comit, Devon

* In a note, quoting from Ford's "Handbook of Spain," Blunt
says "That there is an altar frontal of St. Paul's Cathedral in
use still at Valencia; and a cope from the same church which is
preserved at Zaragosa."

† Incumbents of Somerset (Weaver.)   See App. E.

Incumbent.	Patron.
1533. Rob. Brocke -	- Will. Blount, Exor. test., Ceciliæ, Marchis. de Dorset
1562. Arthur Saul -	- Elizabeth Reg.
1565. Joh. Bridgwater (per recusationem, R. Brock)	- Ex. Coll. Episcopi
1573. Th. Washington in (deprivatione, R. Brock)	Elizabeth Reg.
1580. Th. Wagstaffe -	- Crown
1581. Will. Jones -	- ditto
1589. Fr. Godwyn, M.A.	- ditto
1610. Edw. Coward, S.T.P. -	ditto
1610. Joh. Borbage -	- ditto
1617. Will. Peterson, S.T.P.	ditto
1642. Adam Bellinden, S.T.P.	ditto
1660. Alex. Robinson, M.A.	ditto
1662. Hammet Ward, M.D.	ditto
1672. Will. Mitchel	- ditto
1713. Patric. Mac Donald, M.A.	ditto
1717. Step. Hales, S.T.B. -	ditto
1723. Edw. Passinham, M.A.	ditto
1734. Will. Moggeridge, M.A.	ditto
1763. Arthur Hele, M.A. -	ditto
1783. George Pollen, M.A.	ditto
1818. John Pitman, M.A. -	ditto
1831. A. J. Clarke, M.A. -	ditto
1839. Silvanus Brown	- ditto
1872. Walter Hook, M.A. -	ditto

There is some difficulty in understanding Robert Brock's relations with the parish after his resignation in

1562. It is in that year stated that Arthur Saul was presented to the living on the resignation of Brock (per resignationem). But when John Bridgwater was presented in 1565, it was "per recusationem Rob. Brock," and again when T. Washington was presented in 1573, it was "in deprivatione, R. Brock."

In those days of startling changes, in the reigns of Hen. VIII., Edw. VI., Mary and Elizabeth, it would require the versatility of a Vicar of Bray to enable any one to keep the "even tenour of his way," and Brock apparently failed in this. But the "deprivation" in the last entry may be a mistake. Bridgwater, probably, was the man deprived. And this seems the more likely, as he had to give up his other preferments, and they were numerous about this time. An account of him is given by Anthony Wood, in his "History of the Colleges and Halls of Oxford.* He was elected Rector of Lincoln College, Oxford—the 13th Rector—Aug. 14th, 1563, having been as an undergraduate at Brazenose College. He resigned July 20th, 1574, "to prevent," Wood says, "as I conceive, expulsion." In a note it is added, John Bridgwater, or *Aqua pontanus*, as he writes himself, was admitted in 1562, May 1st, Rector of Wotton Courtney, in the diocese of Wells; and May 23rd, 1563, Rector of Luccombe in the same diocese, being then also Arch-deacon of Rochester; and soon after being made Canon Residentiary of Wells, was admitted Rector of Porlock, n the diocese thereof, April 16th, 1565. In 1570, he was admitted Master of the Hospital of St. Katherine, near Bedminstre, and in 1572, to the prebendal stall of Bishop's Compton, in the Church of Wells. After resigning the Rectorship of this (Lincoln) College he

---

* Vol. I , p 241.

went to Rheimes, where continuing for a time, did at
length (as it is said) enter himself into the Society of
Jesus.   In 1594 he was living at Triers, in Germany; at
all events, he resigned the Rectory of Porlock in 1573.
He wrote several books on controversial subjects, the
titles of two of which will show the bent of his mind.
One was "Concertatio Ecclesiæ Catholica in Anglia,"
published at Triers in 1583; another, "An Account of
the Six Articles, usually proposed to the Missionaries
that suffered in England."

From the dates given in the List of Incumbents, it would
appear that Adam Bellinden, who was presented in 1642,
held the benefice throughout the period of the Commonwealth.   But it was not so.   Dr. Bellinden died in
1647, and was buried at Porlock.   The next year the
register was signed by Alex. Robinson, "Rectore."

Dr. Bellinden had been Bishop of Aberdeen, and was
one of those unfortunate prelates who had to fly from
Scotland in 1639.   On the 22nd of March in that year
the Bishop had left his palace in Old Aberdeen, and
removed to New Aberdeen "for better security."   Here
he preached and administered the Holy Communion, but
on the 27th was compelled, by the threats of the Coven-
anters, to leave the town.   In 1640 he was living in
great poverty in London, but two years later it was
rumoured in Aberdeen that the King had given him a
benefice.   "He survived," says the historian, "till the
month of April, 1642, but died soon afterwards."*   This
we know to be incorrect, for in the old Porlock "Register
of burialls," occurs the entry "Anno Domini 1647,
Martii 4, Adam Bellinden, Dr. of Divinitie and Rector of
Porlock was buryed."

* Lawson's "Episcopal Church of Scotland," p. 611

Alexander Robinson held the living during the time of the Commonwealth after Bishop Bellinden's death. He was an Independent; but as was often the case, was again instituted Rector after the Restoration. But he refused to conform to the Liturgy and Rites of the Church, and so in the year 1662 was ejected.*

In 1717 we find Stephen Hales, Rector of Porlock—a man learned, not in theology, but in botany and anatomy, who was elected a Fellow of the Royal Society in the same year as his presentation to the Rectory of Porlock. He was a Fellow of Benet College, Cambridge, but had the degree of D.D. conferred upon him by the University of Oxford in 1733. He was also perpetual Curate of Teddington, in Middlesex, and Rector of Faringdon, in Hampshire. But his tastes were all scientific, and he resigned the living of Porlock in 1723, and resided at Teddington, where he wrote several works, some of which gained considerable reputation. His " Vegitable Staticks " was translated into French by Buffon, and there are also editions in Italian, German and Dutch. He also wrote on the circulation of the blood in animals, calling his book " Hemastaticks." He was also an inventor, and his ventilator for mines, prisons, hospitals, and the holds of ships, was laid before the Royal Society in 1741, and highly approved.

Dr. Hales was elected one of the eight foreign members of the French Academy of Sciences in 1753 in the place of Sir Hans Sloane. He was offered ecclesiastical promotion notably a canonry at Windsor, but he refused, preferring to spend the days of his old age in seclusion and study at Teddington. After the death of Frederic, Prince of Wales, Dr. Hales was appointed Clerk of the closet to the

---

* " Incumbents of Somerse (Weaver)." p. 421.

Princess Dowager, who had a great respect for him, and erected a monument to his memory in Westminster Abbey (and a very ugly one it is !). He was buried at Teddington, having attained the venerable age of eighty-four.*

One great evil of the times was the permission accorded to one clergyman to hold several livings at the same time. Though this was against the law, yet we find in many cases one person holding four or five benefices together, working them by curates, who were often an inferior class of men. The Rector himself apparently visited his parishes but very rarely. The name of the Rev. Edward Passingham, the successor of Dr. Hales, as Rector of Porlock, does not occur once in the registers, nor does that of Mr. Moggridge, who held the Vicarage of Minehead for fifty-three years, and for twenty-nine years of that time the Rectory of Porlock also. The Churchwardens' book is signed in 1763 and 1764 by the Rev. Arthur Hele, and the registers were signed by him in 1772, but as a rule the Curate, the Rev. D. Williams, seems to have been in charge. He wrote a very good hand. The name of Mr. Hele's successor, Rev. George Pollen, does not appear except in an indenture dated 1806, relating to one of the charities connected with Porlock. He died in 1808, and his successor, the Rev. John Pitman, after his institution, apparently never came near the place. One of the oldest inhabitants, whose memory carries him back to the beginning of this century, says that he never saw Mr. Pitman, nor knew anyone who had : but he remembers the Curate, the Rev. Hugh Passmore, very well. Mr.

---

* Dr. Hales was also the author of an essay entitled "A Friendly Admonition to the Drinkers of Gin, Brandy, and other Spirituous Liquors," which has been several times reprinted.

Passmore lived in the Rectory House. Mr. Pitman died in 1831, and the Rev. A. J. Clarke was presented to the living. He lived in, and greatly improved, the Rectory House.

By the non-residence of Rectors in the last, and at the beginning of this century, a great number of the lands belonging to the Rectory have been lost. The Rector of Porlock is Lord of a Manor. He holds, or used to hold, a court baron, and receive "fines" for putting in fresh lives on the copy-holds, and claiming heriots, etc. All the lands, houses and cottages, were held by copy-hold tenants for lives. There was also a quantity of "waste" or moor land on the manor, on which encroachments were made from time to time, never restrained, and many acres have thus passed away from the church property.

CHAPTER VI.

THE CHURCHWARDENS' CHURCH.

WHAT with the non-residence, both of the lords of the manors and of the rectors, and the power given into the hands of the churchwardens to do whatsoever they pleased, the eighteenth, and first part of the nineteenth century was an evil period for country parish churches Alterations were made; old monuments cut about, and removed; time-honoured erections taken away, or chopped about recklessly; piscinas filled up with rubble, to save expense of repair; the whole "character" of the edifices changed. It may not have been from lack of reverence—it was probably from ignorance and utter want of any artistic feeling on the part of the members of the vestries. Left to themselves, without any guiding or educated influence over them, the ruling principle, the evil demon, was "economy." All that had to be done was to be done as cheaply as possible; there was no further consideration. And so in 1872 the church at Porlock was in a sad state, and though something was done then to remedy the carelessness of past years, yet it was evident that a thorough restoration was necessary. A few points may be observed.

First, we may take the monument of the crusader, Sir Simon Fitz-Roges, the lord of the manor, by whom, as we have seen, the early English Church was erected. This monument is evidently not in its original position. The crusader now lies in an ancient circular niche in the south-western wall. But in order to place him there, his feet, and the lion on which his feet rested, had to be cut off. The lion was missing—it was found at the restoration of the church, built into one of the windows, and cut at the back. One of the crusader's feet also was found when the flooring was taken up to lay down a new pavement on concrete. It has been conjectured that this mutilation took place when Sir John, Lord Harington, founded his beautiful chantry chapel. But it was hardly likely that he should have desecrated the monument of one who was connected with his family, and to whom he would look with reverential memory. Moreover, a plinth, exactly corresponding in length with the crusader's effigy of fifteenth century work, was found in excavating the ground round the walls of the church. It seems therefore more probable that the monument of Sir Simon was repaired by Sir John Harington, or his wife, the Lady Elizabeth, and the plinth added to raise it to a better position. The mutilation took place at a later date—that is, in the "Churchwardens' Church." The work on the back of the lion on which the crusader's feet had rested, and which, as has been said, had been used in repair of one of the window shafts, was certainly of far later date —eighteenth century.

Then with regard to the roof. It is believed that at present we have got the exact shape of the original. But it was only from one beam and rafter that the old form was discovered. In fact, after careful examination, Mr. Sedding had determined upon, and drawn plans for a wagon roof, similar to that in the south aisle. Mr. Huish, one of the contractors for the work, however, found one part which he thought must be of the original shape. Mr. Sedding seized on it with avidity, and the consequence is the beautiful pentagonal roof, probably in exactly the same proportions as that erected in Sir Simon Fitz-Roges' time. But how, from motives of economy, had that roof been treated in the church-wardens' times! Instead of replacing old and decayed rafters and beams with new, the churchwardens had had the old rotten affairs fished and spliced till the whole roof had sunk, and presented a strange and forlorn appearance. It was therefore determined in 1767 to cover it all up so that its deficiencies might not be apparent, real though they were! Accordingly at a public meeting of the churchwardens and the principal inhabitants, it was agreed to ceil the roof of the church, and to do other repairs and amendments upon the said roof as should be deemed necessary by the churchwardens and the under-taker, Mr. Peter Greenwood. He (Mr. P. G.) contracted to ceil and plaister the roof of the said church for the sum of twenty guineas, and to find all necessary materials at his own proper cost and expense, and to bring the same into place, and to lay them up in a workmanlike manner, the churchwardens only to find poles and boards for scaffolding. Mr. Greenwood also engaged to keep up and repair the ceiling and roof inside for twenty years without any further charge.*

So much work for so little money! No wonder that the beams were spliced with elm instead of oak, and that in the most meagre manner. It is a marvel that the rafters kept together as long as they did, but there is no doubt that the roof was in a dangerous condition years before the restoration.

There was in the olden times a Screen of which traces may still be seen in the steps in the wall leading to the loft, and the marks in the pillars where the Screen went.

---

* Churchwardens' Accounts, 1767.

The top of it was also discovered worked as a prop into the old gallery. It was richly carved and coloured. It might no doubt have been repaired, but that would have been expensive, so without any public meeting it was removed *in toto*, and the following entry appears in the accounts, "paid to James Taylor for ale when ye Seren was taken down 1s."* Other work was equally ruthless. The beautiful Early English Arch at the west was filled up in order that a gallery might be placed in front of it, and a hole was knocked in the roof at the side to insert a window of the real Churchwarden type. The parvise was turned into a lumber room, and the spiral staircase leading to it was filled up with rubble. A hole was knocked in the outside wall to enable the sexton to put into the quaint old room rubbish he could not stack away elsewhere. The mullions of the windows were repaired with wood instead of stone, except where such a "find" as the lion of the Crusader could be utilized! The fine monument of Sir John and Lady Elizabeth Harington was left in a disgraceful condition, a few iron bars put here and there, only serving to corrode the stone, and make bad worse, and (*horresco referens*) through the mouth of the effigy of Sir John a deep hole had been chiselled to support some bar or pole.† The decorated north east window in the chancel was filled up, and also the beautiful piscina, in order that a mural monument might be placed there. Of course high pews had been erected, and also a lofty "three decker," and there was at the east end a large black board, as a reredos, containing in gilt letters the

* Churchwardens' Accounts, 1768.

† This splendid monument has been restored and the missing parts supplied, in exact imitation, by Mr John Cooksley.

9

Creed, the Lord's Prayer, the Ten Commandments, and the names of the churchwardens.

The monument in the chancel referred to has been placed against the north side of the wall in the Tower. It is of stone and black marble and was originally much painted and gilded. It was erected to the memory of the late Rev. Nathaniel Arundel, S.T.B., Rector of Exford, who died in 1705, by his widow, the eldest daughter of the Rev. W. Mitchell, Rector of Porlock. The coat of arms shows his connection with the Arundel family, and the Latin inscription testifies that as a pastor, a husband, a friend to the poor, and a champion of the church, none could be found his equal.

The entry of his burial in the Porlock Register has this remark appended to it, " It is not known what Mr. Arundel died worth."

The estimated "worth" of a man or a woman is often put down in the register, such as—"Jan 3rd. 1703, Joan Chibbett, buried in woollen only. Joan Chibbett was worth but little." All the entries from 1678 to 1713 have the note added "buried in woollen only."

"Briefs" used to be sent to parishes throughout England. The word is used in our Prayer Book, and such "briefs" were to be read among the notices after the Nicene Creed. They, under the Sovereign's Letters Patent, authorized a collection for a charitable purpose, and were called King's or Queen's letters. They were very general in the 17th century, and in most parish registers mention of them is made. In the Porlock Register we find such as these : "*Anno Domini* 1662, collected for the Protestant churches in Lithuania, whose deputy was John Kramo Kramski, 8s. 8d. ; left in the hands of Andrew Kent, H.C." Or for individuals—as " for Mrs. Darmond, the wife of Dr. Darmond in

Ireland, 5s."; for the "sad fire in London"; for the "redemption of slaves in Algeria"; and for many objects, some important, some apparently trivial, briefs were sent out. None however have been issued since 1854.

The Churchwardens' Accounts for Porlock only date back to 1736. That there was an older book there can be no doubt. But the parish books were kept, or, rather, not kept, in a most careless manner. The old register dating back to 1618 was found in a loft in 1845 in the house of Mr. H. Phelps, a substantial yeoman, of whose family several members had been churchwardens. It had been ill-used, burnt, and mutilated, but the remains are now in the church safe. Other books may have existed, which were not forthcoming at that time, and probably never will be.

In the Churchwardens' Accounts are many amusing entries. It appears that they could do pretty much what they liked, from paying for church repairs, and officers salaries, down to remuneration for killing a stoat! For the slaughter of a fox, 3s. 4d. was the regular payment, but he who killed a polecat received only 6d.; and "fitchets" were only valued at 3d. For killing a fittahot 4d. was given; but this entry only occurs twice, and it is not known what a "fittahot" was. One Thomas Grey received a shilling for killing a "grig," whatever that might imply.* But against fitchets and hedgehogs† were the chief forays. In 1754, £1 10s. 6d. was given for "killing fitchets and hedgehogs," and at another time

---

* A "grig" is a sand eel, but, as sand eels do not exist at Porlock, it seems probable that the 1/- was given for the destruction of a large viper or a snake.

† The innocent hedgehog was supposed to suck the milk of the cows, when they were lying down.

10s. was allowed for sixty-two hedgehogs, and in 1758 £1 2s. 10d. was given "to sundrie people for killing 137 hedgehogs."

The Holy Communion was celebrated four times, or sometimes five times, a year, and the charge for wine and for bread is duly entered. But the amount for the former—two gallons of Tent or Tynte wine, at £1 10s. to £2 10s.—seems a large order for so few occasions.

But the parishioners in vestry were careful in other respects. At visitation, a word which caused considerable difficulty to the scribe, as it is spelt "vitastion," "visit-stion," "visation," and in other ways, the "passon" and churchwardens seem to have charged too much. So there is an entry in April, 1755, thus:—"An agrosment made by the farmers of the parish of Porlock hoart (? whereby) the churchwardens are to expend at the two visitatiuns, and the charge of the court and the parson's dinner with it, we do think proper to allow them one guinea and no more. Witness our hands." There are eleven signatures and only one "mark."

This rule however was not afterwards insisted upon. In the time of Mr. Passmore, evidently a very popular curate, who lived in the Rectory House during the non-residence of Mr. Pitman, the Rector, who never came near the place, the "parson" was allowed 10s., 12s. 6d., and even 15s. for his dinner !

The surplice too was an expensive matter. In 1763 a charge is made for 12¾ yards of holland, at 3s. 10d. per yard, £2. 9s.; and for making the "surplis," 5/-. The size of the surplice would seem to have been traditional, as in other entries exactly the same quantity of holland is mentioned. The price in 1788 was 3s. 11d. per yard.

The vestry, however, seemed to be careful of the spire, and entries for wood and pegs for its repair are frequent.

There was a considerable "restoration" apparently in 1787, when there is an entry of payment to "Mr. Baker, of Bamton, for 4,008 spindells at £1 8s. per thousand, with carriage £5 12s." Next year we have, "paid James Chilcott's bill for labour in repairing the church and steeple, £9 7s. 6d." And then of course there was the beer to be considered, and the cost was entered on the vestry book, "paid for ale when the cradle was histed, 3s." The "histing of the cradle" is not mentioned elsewhere in the parish accounts, but no doubt it was frequently used. It implied a cage, or small platform which was drawn up from the top, in which a man stood to repair the outside, at whatever part required. There are persons now living who remember this being done, but it came to be neglected some sixty years ago. The shales or shingles are of oak, twelve by four inches in size, and are fitted over each other. Inside there is a good specimen of early English work, the beams being beautifully built and fitted together. The tower itself, low, broad and very substantial, may have been, as we have said, part of a rather older building. But the wooden spire is not of much later date, and was probably erected in the time of Sir Simon Fitz-Roges. It is a quaint structure, and all the more so as it is at present truncated. When the top was removed there is no evidence to tell us. Savage says it was blown off about the year 1700, but this was mere hearsay. According to others it was struck by lightning. The latter idea cannot be entertained, as the effect of a lightning stroke would have been downwards, and there is no trace of this. It very likely was blown off, but a good reason has been suggested for its not having been rebuilt. It was probably used as a beacon, from which a fire, or a torch displayed, might guide the fishing boats to harbour; and this is the more likely as it is in a position from whence it would be mos useful. However, when the spire was restored in 1884, it was left in the old form, for as it was pertinently said by one whose advice was asked, "You can see a spire with a point anywhere, but *this* is peculiar to Porlock."

In 1884 there were holes in the sides, all the shales were more or less rotten, and small repairs would be of no avail. So it was taken in hand, and under the direction and supervision of Mr. Samson, architect, the inner timbers were strengthened, and the whole of the outside stripped and recovered with oaken shales.

There are five bells, in the key of G minor. On the first one is the inscription, "*Life is death and death is life*, 1617." On the second, ": I : I.: I am the se cond bel, T.P., D.S., 1617."

The others are dated 1801, 1823, and 1782 respectively, and bear the names of the churchwardens.*

In 1802 the first bell was recast. The entry is "for casting ye first bell, for additional mittel 1 cwt. 2 qrs. 21 lbs., and wasting mettle of the old bell in melting down, 22 lbs. at 16s. 8d. = £21 3s. 4d." It is to be hoped that the metal was better than the spelling.

The tenor bell was recast in 1824 at Cullompton at a cost of £45 15s.; with charge of carriage to and from Cullompton of £3.†

The bells were much used; ringing is provocative of much thirst, and numerous are the entries "ale for ye ringers." On the 5th of November and on other "days of rejoicing," *i.e.* the 29th of May, the anniversary of the King or Queen's accession to the throne, etc., 10s. was

---

* "Church bells of Somerset," H. J. Ellacombe, 1874. Halliday's Monuments.

† Churchwardens' Accounts, 1824

the sum allowed. On extra occasions the allowance
appears to have been according to the importance of the
event. When there came "extraordinary newes from the
King" 1758-9—probably the great victory of Admiral
Hawke and Lord Howe over the French at Quiberon
Bay—5s. were given. On the "rejoicing day for taking
Quebick and other segnell victories over enemies" 18s.
was the sum allowed. The King's "crownation days" were
thirsty ones. In 1762 £2 4s. 5d. was the ringers' allowance;
in 1822 and 1832 £1 only. But in fairness it must be
stated that the ringers were not the only droughty ones.
At every extra job, in or about the church—as for
instance the laying the foundation of the church wall;
or "righting ye gollery" (1748)—ale was allowed, but
reckoned for, we suppose, in the wages.

The churchwardens relieved many poor persons with
the ratepayers' money. "Pore travelers"; "travelors from
turkey"; "many poor prissoners of war in all this year
(1745)"; "pore travelers with passes," etc., received help.

The Rev. J. Clarke, who was appointed rector in 1831,
was the first resident rector for certainly 100 years.
At the very first meeting, the rector in the chair, it was
determined that certain repairs should be done to the
church, and Mr. W. Horne was requested to give an
estimate. This amounted to £115; but there is no
record as to whether it was collected or expended. At
the same meeting it was ordered that no accounts should
be passed by the vestry "unless they were receipted and
the items specified for what purpose employed, and
proper dates to the several accounts." Still the various
accounts were *not* dated afterwards. A list of instru-
ments of music belonging to the parish was also entered.
It is a meagre one. There was one flute and one
violoncello, held by John and Nicolas Foy!

The spire, as has been said, was restored in 1884. At a parish meeting held on August 30th, 1888, it was unanimously resolved "that the renovation of the roof, and other structural repairs, at present absolutely necessary, should be taken in hand as soon as possible." A committee was at once formed, with Mrs. Hook as Hon. Sec. and Treasurer. Mr. Sedding and Mr. Samson were appointed architects. After examination it was stated that the necessary repairs would cost £970 at least : but that it was further desirable that the old West Arch which had been closed when the gallery was erected should be opened out; that the church should be reseated; and that the existing vestry, which was in a very dilapidated condition, should be restored. This would bring up the cost to £1,270. Finding that one part of the walls—at the north east end—was too much decayed to be available, Mr. Sedding proposed that an organ chamber and choir vestry should be built there. The committee in their circular stated that "no further changes in the fabric of the Church are contemplated, it being unanimously agreed that it is to the last degree undesirable, under the pretence of 'Restoration,' to detract in any way from the historical and artistic interest which it is admitted to possess."

Fancy fairs, sales of work, etc., were held at the Rectory and in the Rectory field, under a ladies' committee, and in less than two years the state of the finances warranted a commencement, though the original estimate was exceeded by £500. The church was closed on May 5th, 1890, and the services were carried on in the schoolroom, and a church room specially fitted up and licensed. The contractors were Messrs. Huish & Cooksley, and it is a matter for the parish to be proud of, that all the work was carried out by Porlock men. There was no delay.

On May 28th, 1891, the church was re-opened by the Lord Bishop of the Diocese, the Right Rev. and Right Hon. Lord Arthur Charles Hervey. Nearly all the clergy of the Deanery assembled to meet his lordship and to take part in the services. It was indeed a day of thanksgiving when, restored to its ancient beauty, was again dedicated to the honour and glory of God, the Church of St. Dubricius.

CHAPTER VII

THE CHURCHYARD AND CHAPELS.

THE old churchyard of Porlock was ordered to be closed by the Queen in Council in 1889. A year's grace was allowed to enable the parishioners to provide another burial ground, and a spot was selected up the Hawkcombe valley, not a quarter of a mile to the south of the church. This was consecrated by the Lord Bishop of the Diocese on February 19th, 1891. It is a beautiful site, and has the advantage of being near enough to the Church and Wesleyan Chapel to dispense with the necessity of chapels being built. In the old churchyard there are several quaint epitaphs, some of which display a little confusion in grammatical construction, as for example :—

" Cease now, dear friends, and weep no more,
I are not dead, but gone before :
Like as the bud nipt of the tree,
So death have parted you and me."

1780.

" My dearest Friends advised be,
Weep for yourselves and not for we ;
These and these only who do this
Will gain eternal Joy and Bliss."

1783.

" Long time in pain we did remain
While o'er world's plain we trod,
But now we're free, death eased we,
And glory be to God."

1834.

" Within this grave there here doth lie
Four children of mortality,
Who in their youth, and in their prime
God thought it fit, the only time
To take them hence Him to adore,
And sing His praise for evermore.
Dear parents now contented be,
We are like buds nipt of the tree :
Comfort yourselfs and be content,
And souls with Christ do not lament."

The poetical idea of being " nipt of the tree " is repeated many times, and the ground of contentment is also urged more than once upon the sorrowing survivors. The poetic fancy of the composer was somewhat constrained by the limits of previous epitaphs

" When death was sent from God above
So suddenly to part our love ;
No friends, nor yet physician's art
Could then prevent His fatal dart.
Comfort yourself and be content,
A soul with Christ do not lament."

1790.

On the grave of a husband and wife who died within a day of each other there is a headstone with this pathetic inscription :—

" He first departed, she for one day tried to live without him,
liked it not and died."

A grand old yew tree still overshadows the church path. It is decrepit from age, and its branches have to be propped up, yet spring after spring it shows signs of vitality. The ancient churchyard cross, supported by three steps, still remains, but is not in good condition.

There is a structure at the west of the church porch, richly carved, with the emblems of the Passion in a shield in front, and a portcullis on the east end. This has been supposed to have been an altar tomb. But Mr. E. Buckle suggests, with great probability, that it was a dole stone, or stone on which the alms of benefactors were distributed, examples of which may be seen in many places. They are generally placed between the churchyard gate and the church porch. There is one in the neighbouring churchyard of Selworthy, but not so ornate. These structures may have been used for other religious purposes. Perhaps originally they were tombs, as they seem always to lie east and west, and were utilized, being placed in a convenient position for the dole-giving. It may be that future investigations will throw some light on the subject. To the east of the churchyard runs the Chantry Lane, and in it is a building called "Chantry Cottage." It is, however, of earlier date than the foundation of the chantry, in fact both tradition and the timbers point to the twelfth or early part of the thirteenth century as the time of its erection. Perhaps it was an old dwelling-house given by Lady Elizabeth for the use of the two chantry priests.

The ancient Manor House is at Worthy, to the west of Porlock Weir. In 1830 it was "improved," and but few traces remain of the old house. The principals of the roof, made of oak with elm supports, are old, and the large hall fireplace remains. On the staircase there is a hiding place, but whether ever used or not there is no tradition to tell. Two chimney pieces of alabaster were very likely made at the time when the alabaster effigies of Sir John and Lady E. Harington were ordained for the church. There was another manor house of small dimensions near the church of Porlock, but in the parish of Luccombe. It was in Doverhay, or as it more properly should be spelt "Dovery." In Domesday book it is said of this manor :—"Alric holds from Roger (de Corcelle) Dovri," and in the Exeter book it is spelt Doveri In the time

of Edward the Confessor it was held by a certain Lady
Edith. This was not Queen Edith, who, as before mentioned, held the Manor of Selworthy, but an Edith, or
Edeva, of whom nothing is known. Her Norman successor was Roger de Courcelle.* The size and value
of the manor do not come under our consideration ; but
the fact of Dovery being so near Porlock gave rise to a
curious mistake, the Church of Porlock being called, at
one time, the church of Doverhay.

In early days the first fruits and tenths of all ecclesiastical benefices were paid to the Pope of Rome. In 1253
Innocent IV. granted these for three years to Henry III.,
which caused a taxation report to be made, which is
called the " Norwich taxation," or Pope Innocent's
" valor." In 1288 Pope Nicolas made a similar grant to
Edward I. for six years towards defraying an expedition
to the Holy Land. That the full value might be obtained,
the king issued a precept for a fresh return of taxation,
which was not completed till 1291 in the province of
Canterbury. It was carried out under the supervision of
John, Bishop of Winchester, and Oliver, Bishop of
Lincoln.† In this survey the church of Doverhay is
entered with the sum of £8 6s. 8d. against it-- the
highest value of all the churches in the deanery of Dunster.
It is evident that this was a mistake, as there are no
records or traces of a church in Dovery. But it was a
natural, if careless, mistake, as the two manors are
separated only by a small stream which runs close to
the east of Porlock Church.

The Manor House of Dovery is now in the possession

---

* Eyton's Domesday Studies, i. 83.
† Caley's preface to Pope Nicolas' Taxation   Record Commi-
sioners, fol. 1802.   Savage's Carhampton, p. 41

of Mr. Chadwyck Healey, Q.C., and is being restored under the supervision of Mr. E. Buckle to whom I am indebted for the following account.

"The house appears to have been built in the latter part of the fifteenth century, or early in the sixteenth. It is interesting as an example of a remarkably small manor house of that date. Though hardly more than a cottage in size, in style and finish it is not inferior to many a larger house.

"The hall is only 18ft. long by 13ft. 6in. wide, but it has a handsome oak ceiling, and stone fireplace, and a large and richly traceried window. This window is four lights wide, with a square head; it is crossed by a transom, having two tiny quatrefoils over each light, a favourite arrangement in the south and west of Somerset; and the head is filled with tracery of a rare and quaint design, the characteristic feature of which is that the cusped arch at the top of each light is incomplete (appearing as though the point of the arch had been cut away), and the glass runs up without a break into the central batement light over. Similar tracery may be seen in the south aisle of Old Cleeve Church, and in the east window of Queen Camel (for the chancel of which Cleeve Abbey was responsible), in the west window at Wellington,—and in two windows at Holcombe Rogus in Devonshire,—the east window of the chancel, and the east window of the south aisle. Holcombe Rogus is within five miles of Wellington, and is named after the family of Roges before referred to, one of whom bought Dovery in 1236, but it had before this passed to the Bluetts, and it seems improbable that the architectural similarity is due to this connection. But there was another family tie which may possibly have brought it about; for William Lord Harington, brother and heir of the knight of the Porlock monument, married a daughter of Sir John Halle (or Hyll) of Kyton in Holcombe.

"Over the hall is a chamber approached by a stone vice, which has an open roof of oak, a small fireplace of perhaps later date, and four small windows destitute of tracery. The arrangement of the windows in the north gable points to the conclusion that another roof always abutted against this end of the house, but the existing building in this position is quite modern. Probably its predecessor contained the solar.

"The south wing is of nearly the same date as the central portion. This seems to have been intended for the kitchen offices, and to have had bedrooms over, approached by a separate vice, in the position now occupied by the porch to one of the cottages."

Both Dovery and Porlock were in a state of excitement three times a year, when the May, August and October fairs were held. At the last there were sometimes as many as 1500 sheep and 200 bullocks "penned" in the street. There were also weekly markets, when the farmers and their wives from the hill country sold their produce. There was a market house and a market cross—but where are they now? They were probably destroyed in the careless age—at the beginning of this century. The barn in which the hurdles were kept, and was dignified by the name of "Market House," and was converted into a dwelling house in 1880, was certainly not the old market house. In a linhay not far off there are some oak posts which would seem to have been originally designed for some higher purpose—a "saddle stone" of an old cross has been found hard by; a carved oak dolphin, obtained from a Porlock man, is to be seen at Glenthorne—tradition speaks of a beautiful market house. Such indirect witnesses tell a tale of destruction and spoliation.

An old inhabitant, one John Ward, who died in 1873 at the age of eighty-three, told the writer that he could remember a market house something like that at Dunster, and other aged persons have heard their fathers speak of the same.

This John Ward lived in a cottage which was known by the name of the Chapel Cottage. There were traces of an old and ornamental chapel in the walls, in the windows, and in the roof. Moreover, two piscinas were discovered there. There was evidently an old building for worship, and, judging from the first piscina, part of it, which may be called the nave, was older than the rest. A chancel, or perhaps a chantry was added, and in this was placed the second piscina, which is of more recent construction. When the Chapel of Ease was erected in 1874, entreaties were made to the lord of the manor to allow the restoration of this old fabric, but the cottage into which it had been turned was not then available, and since that the whole has been done away with, and a dwelling house erected on the site. The piscinas are built into the wall of this house. Fortunately Mr. Samson, F.R.I.B.A., obtained some drawings of the old building, which he still possesses, and photographs were taken by Mr. Chadwyck Healey, Q.C. The engravings here given are from those photographs and show what the old chapel was.

There are other chapels in the neighbourhood which may have been served from Cleeve Abbey; one at Lynch in the parish of Selworthy, about a mile to the north east from Porlock church, which had been used as a barn, has been restored and refitted by the Right Hon. Sir T. D. Acland, Bart. The foundations of another very small chapel may be seen about three-quarters of a mile to the south of Holnicote house. A track down the hill at the

east of the Horner valley is still known by the name of the " Priest's path," from which we may suppose, without improbability, the priest wended his way from the chapel in the valley to a church—most likely Stoke Pero—on the hill. A lovely walk he would have, and from the top of the hill would see right away from Hurtstone point to the east, to Culbone woods to the west, with Wales in front of him. Leland in his Itinerary (Vol. II.) mentions this bay prosaically thus :—" From Minheved doune on the Severne shore to a place called Hores-Toun, a three miles. There beginnith the Rode that is communely caullid Porlogh Bay, a meatly good Rode for Shippes, and so goith to Comban, peraventure shortely spoken for Columbane, a three miles of ; and thus far I was adcertenid that Somersetshir went on farther."

Southey resting on his way to Glenthorne from a visit to Coleridge in his beautiful home "on seaward Quantock's heathy hills," and taking shelter at the old Ship Inn at Porlock, writes more poetically :—

" Porlock! thy verdant vale, so fair to sight,
Thy lofty hills with fern and furze so brown,
The waters that so musical roll down
Thy woody glens, the traveller with delight
Recalls to memory, and the channel grey,
Circling it, surges in thy level bay.
Porlock, I also shall forget thee not,
Here by the unwelcome summer rain confined,
And often shall hereafter call to mind
How here, a patient prisoner, 'twas my lot
To wear the lonely lingering close of day,
Making my sonnet by the alehouse fire,
Whilst idleness and solitude inspire
Dull rhymes to pass the duller hours away."

APPENDIX.

APPENDIX A.

THE ancient wild songs referred to are those of the bards Aneurin, Taliesin, Lly-warch Hên, and Merddyn. They are published in the "Myvyrian Archaiology of Wales," Lond., 1801-7. For their date see Turner's Hist. of Ang. Sax. The works of Gildas (born A.D. 516), and the supposed works of Nennius (with regard to which see Turner Vol. i., p. 201; and Lappenberg Hist. of Ang. Sax., Vol. I., xxvii.) were published by the Eng. Hist. Soc. in 1838; and there are other transla-tions by Giles (1841); Todd and Herbert (Irish Arch. Soc., 1848) etc. Bede (born A.D. 673) cites Gildas and surnames him "the wise." He does not say much of Dubricius; and the Annales Cambriæ only give the date of the saint's death (A.D. 612). The tales collected by Geoffry or Jeffry ap Arthur of Monmouth, in his "Chronicon sive Historia Britonum," which he professes to have translated from a British Chronicle called "Brut y Brenhined," have caused much controversy from the earliest times, some of the con-temporary Chroniclers, such as William of Newburgh, Giraldus Cambrensis, and William of Malmesbury, going against Jeffry. The other side is given, amongst others, in the preface to the "Chronicle of Caradoc," by H. Wynne. Jeffry, of course, refers to Dubricius in his connection with King Arthur (Bk. VIII., c. 2; Bk. IX., c.c. 1-12, etc.), but it is difficult to separate the historical from the fabulous. The Llandaff book was edited for the Welsh M. S. S. Soc. by the Rev. W. J. Rees, with an English translation, 1840. A life of St. Dubricius, by Benedict, of Gloucester, who wrote after Jeffry, of Monmouth, is contained in Wharton's Anglia Sacra (ii. 654, seq.); where is also given an anonymous "life" ii. 667) which appears to have been compiled from earlier sources than the fables of Jeffry. There is also a "life" in

Capgrave's ' Nova Legenda Angliæ" (F. 87). With regard
to the Llandaff bishopric, and Dubricius' connection with
Erchenfield, reference must be made to Haddan and Stubbs
(Councils, i. 146) ; and for the early and legendary succes-
sions to Llandaff and Caerleon to Stubbs' Registrum 154,
155.

Rees (Welsh Saints, pp. 144, 170, etc.) gives an interesting
account of the Saint, but he follows Jeffry, of Monmouth, in
his dates, and buries Dubricius in 522. Canon Bright, while
rejecting these dates, cannot believe in the extreme old age
given to Dubricius in the Llandaff book. Still, with the
records of old Parr and Henry Jenkins before us, we may
assert that it is not impossible that Dubricius crowned King
Arthur, and yet died in 612.

APPENDIX B.

IN Domesday the arable land is estimated in " carucates,"
the pasture in " hides," the meadows and woods in acres.
The measure of the carucate—or land which one carruca
or team of oxen (probably eight) could plough in the year
—varied at different times, and in different places ; as, of
course, a great deal depended on the nature of the soil,
In one Charter of Richard I, the carucate was estimated
at 60 acres, in another at 100.   In 23, Edw. III, in one
place a carucate was valued at 112 acres, and in a neighbouring Manor at 150.   So also with regard to " hides "—
the word implying a homestead or settlement of one family.
The size varied according to the quality of the land, and
local considerations.   Thus the average size in Domesday
for Somerset generally was 250 acres ; but in the Hundred
of Carhampton it was as much as 973 acres. At Porlock the
hide would seem to have been about 320 acres. For the
value was, as a rule, a penny per acre (though sometimes
twopence or more), and the three hides at the penny rate
would give exactly the four pounds mentioned. The fall in
value mentioned in the Exon Domesday, must have been
due to local circumstances—bad farming, or such like. (See
Eyton's Domesday Studies). The Exeter Domesday con-

tains the accounts of the Fegadri or tax collectors for the Gheld for Somerset, which were gathered probably in 1086. After Domesday we have the " Hundred Rolls," which were the returns to writs sent to the Sheriffs, to discover the loss to the Crown arising from negligence in the troubled reign of Henry III. These have been printed by the Record Commission. The " Feet of Lines," " Kirby's Quest " (for Somerset), the " Nomina Villarum," the " Tax Rolls," which are classed in the Record Office as " Exchequer Lay Subsidies " (with an interesting preface by the late F. H. Dickenson), the " Register of John de Drokensford," Bishop of Bath and Wells 1303-29, edited by Bishop Hobhouse ; and the " Somerset Chantries " are printed by the Somerset Record Society.

Appendix C.

PORLOCK.—Two Chauntries within the Parish Church there.

Rents of Assize, and Free Rents in Ugborowe, in the county of Devon, per annum xiii £ xv^d.

Rent of all tenements held at will, according to the custom of the Manor of Ugborowe, per annum, vi £ ii^d.

Rent of a Messuage, with divers other Cottages in Porlocke, demised by copy per annum lxvi^s.

Rent of a dwelling-place called the two Chauntries, with a garden, per annum v^s.

Total   xxiii £ vi^s. iid.

Deduction.—Rent Resolute to the Rector of the Parish Church there, per annum   iiij½^d.

Money paid annually to the same Rector for an acre of land there   ij^s. vi^d.

Rent Resolute to John Arundell, Esquire, of Trevyse, for land in Porlocke, as the price of two capons annually   vij

Money paid for a fee to the Steward holding the court there annually by the foundation   xiij^s. iv^d.

Total   xvi^s. ix½.

And remains over per annum   xxii £. ix^s. iiij½^d.

Land and possession granted to the use and maintenance of a lamp perpetually burning in the parish church there.

John Goulde, junr., holds a house there, and renders
per annum   iiij^x.

It will be observed that sometimes mention is made of two
Chantries, sometimes only of one. In the "Valor Ecclesiasticus" two Chantries are entered, whereas in the inventory
of 37 Hen. VIII., "Our Lady Chantry in Porlock" only is
to be found. It may have been that when W. England, one
of the Chantry Priests, died or left, his Chantry was not
filled up, or the two were held by Robert Laurance. But
this is not probable, as the two Chantries appear again in
1 Edw. VI. It would seem that the discrepancy arose from
a mistake. There were two Chantry Priests, and, therefore,
the Commissioners might take it for granted that there were
two Chantries. They were not bound to be very accurate
in the general reports, while with regard to the inventory
there would be more care. There were never more than
two Chantry Priests at one time at Porlock, and that was
the number authorized for the Harington Chantry. This we
gather from the Baron's will, and from the Patent Rolls
(14 Edw. IV.), where the Royal Licence is given " to found
and establish a perpetual Chantry of two Chaplains, to
celebrate Divine Service at the Altar in the Chapel of the
Blessed Mary in the Parish Church of St. Dubricius in
Porlok, for the well being of the King, and for the souls of,"
etc. There is no trace of a second Chantry.

Appendix D.

It has been supposed, from similarity in the names, that
the Rogers family were descended from the Roges', or
Fitz-Roges', who were lords of the manor in the 13th
century. But there seems to be no ground for this supposition. The first Rogers of eminence was Edward, who was
" comptroller of the Sovereign ladye the Queen's Majestie "
in Queen Elizabeth's reign. He was knighted in 1548. Like
Sir Walter Raleigh, he had beautiful clothes, "gownes of
damask furred with foxe," etc., which he left to his sons;
he died on May 21, 1567. His heir was George, who was
also knighted, and who, besides Cannington and Pilton, had

the Manors of West Pennard and Kingsbury; his will was proved Nov. 6, 1582. Mary, the heiress, who married Sir G. Wynter, was the second daughter of Edward Rogers the second, the son of the above-mentioned George. The eldest was Jane, who married Sir F. Hyde, of Wembury, Devon. The third, Ann, married Paul Methuen, Preb. of Wells. There appear to have been two other daughters, Ellinor, wife of John Huddie, Esq., and Penelope. It was this Edward who acquired from the crown the manors of Porlock and "Borsington," which he left to his son George, his eldest son being Sir Francis Rogers, Kt. Will proved Nov. 19, 1627.

Somersetshire Wills, 2nd series, p. 92.
Bushe's Extinct Baronetcies, 253.

APPENDIX E.

BESIDES the Incumbents we find mention made of several Curates of Porlock, chiefly as witnesses of Wills. Thus in 1533, "Dominus Joh Jackson, Curatus," witnessed the Wills of John Kentle and John Symon ; and in 1536 of John Coppe.⁰ In 1538, Sir Henry Puggisley was Curate of Porlock, and two years later of Selworthy. In 1542, Sir N. Hampton, Curate, witnessed the Will of Robert Zullye, and the year after of William Yeole.† In the same year Sir Marys ffine (Fyne) was also Curate, and as such witnessed the Will of Christopher Mollonde, who left to the Church of Porlock, iiis. ivd., and to Exford, xiid. "for the glasynge of their wyndowes." He left "to my son James and his children II pannes and XIX sylver spones, to hold for me a yearly obett." The "summa Inventarii" was £23 19s. 1d.‡ In 1544, Sir Davyd Condo was Curate,§ and afterwards Sir W. Briford.‖ Between that time and 1625, I have not found the names of any Curates, but in the latter year came

---

* Weaver's "Wells Wills," p. 130.   † Taunton Registry of Wills.
‡ District Probate Registry, Wells (hitherto unpublished), communicated to me by Rev. F W. Weaver. Fyne's name also occurs in the Taunton Registry of Wills.
§ Dist Prob Reg , at Supra   ‖ Taunton Registry of Wills.

Thomas May, who signed the old Porlock Register yearly till 1641. He was succeeded by Robert Blake, who signed the Registers till 1645, and after him came B. Hawkins, who only signed in 1646.

An interesting fact with regard to the Wills which are extant, and have been published by Mr. Weaver, is the reference to "stores." The "store" (instaurum or staurum) was a gild (yeld) or brotherhood, and the Wills show that in some Parishes such associated bodies were numerous. They had, it would seem, in some cases, their Warden, their balance sheet, their audit day and feast day, and, of course, their particular rules. Dulverton had 12 such "stores," Cutcombe and Winsford each 9, Wootton Courtenay 6.* In Porlock there were the "stores' of S. Saviour, S. Olave, S. Dubricius, the Blessed Mary, and the High Cross, besides the Chantry, which had its "bedmen" or "bedemen"—persons who received alms on condition of praying for the soul of the founder. There is a Will of one of these, N. Tolman, "off ye parishe off Luccombe, pore bedman of the chantre of Porloke."† In 1533, one John Upyngton leaves legacies to different "stores"—"in staurum Ecclesie de Porloke," "ad staurum salvatoris aput Porloke," and "ad staurum S. Olavi." John Kentte leaves "instauro S. Dubricii, instauro B.M., instauro S. Olavi (cuilibet) unam ovem." John Holl de Porlocke (1535) mentions the "staurum eccl. de P" in his Will, and John Coppe leaves a small sum "alte cruci," also to "S. Olavo intra parochiam predictam.‡ In some of these Wills the name Dubricius appears as Deverock. Thus John Elsworthye, in 1538, left "unto Saynt Deverockis store two shepe." "This,' Mr. Weaver writes to me, "is evidently the Anglicized form of Dubricius, and is very interesting. There is the parish of S. Devereux, between Hereford and Abergavenny, and when I pass its station in the train it always reminds me of your Patron Saint, after whom of course it is named, S. Dubricius."

---

* Preface to Weaver's " Wells Wills,' pp. vi. xi
† "Wells Wills," p. 101.   ‡ Weaver s "Wells Wills,' p 130.

Appendix F.

LETTERS Patent were granted A.D. 1614 to Edward Roger, Esq., containing licence to hold a market within his Manor of Porlock on Thursday in every week, and also two fairs within the said Manor, each to last for three days; the one on the Eve, the Feast, and the Morrow of St. Barnabas the Apostle; and the other on the Eve, the Feast, and the Morrow of St. Martin in Winter; together with a court of pied-powdre at the time of the said markets and fairs (Patent Roll, 11 James I., Part 13, No. 10).

INDEX.

37

www.ingramcontent.com/pod-product-compliance
Lightning Source LLC
Chambersburg PA
CBHW032110010726
47493CB00008B/2523